"Do they teach you to kiss like that in police school?" she whispered, running her fingers lightly across his lips.

"Basic Interrogation 101," he said.

"I bet you aced the class."

He smiled to himself, and not just because the conversation was silly, but because the sound of her voice did that to him.

"I'm sorry I pointed a gun at you," she said with a quick upsweep of her lashes. "Is it really empty?"

"Yep. That's why I didn't take it with me when I went outside to scout."

"I thought you'd forgotten it."

"Cops don't forget their weapons," he said. But being around her was causing him to forget so many other things, including all the reasons he should stay away from her.

SHATTERED

—

ALICE SHARPE

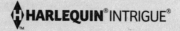

Recycling programs
for this product may
not exist in your area.

This book is dedicated to my delightful friend
and other daughter, Charmian Lodjic,
who loves herself a good cowboy.
Happy reading, honey.

ISBN-13: 978-0-373-69768-7

SHATTERED

Copyright © 2014 by Alice Sharpe

Printed in U.S.A.

www.Harlequin.com

ABOUT THE AUTHOR

Alice Sharpe met her husband-to-be on a cold, foggy beach in Northern California. One year later they were married. Their union has survived the rearing of two children, a handful of earthquakes registering over 6.5, numerous cats and a few special dogs, the latest of which is a yellow Lab named Annie Rose. Alice and her husband now live in a small rural town in Oregon, where she devotes the majority of her time to pursuing her second love, writing.

Alice loves to hear from readers. You can write her c/o Harlequin Books, 233 Broadway, Suite 1001, New York, NY 10279. An SASE for reply is appreciated.

Books by Alice Sharpe

CAST OF CHARACTERS

Nate Matthews—This Arizona deputy sheriff's life changed the day he failed to save those for whom he felt responsible. Little did he know at the time that he was standing on the edge of a devious plot to undermine a nation. He has a chance for redemption now; all he has to do is keep a mysterious woman alive long enough to figure out her true agenda.

Sarah Donovan—Beautiful, enigmatic, frustrated and scared out of her mind. She meets Nate at the worst possible moment in her life. Torn between conflicting goals, she fights her need for and attraction to the man in the black Stetson who seems hell-bent on helping her—whether she wants him to or not.

Mike Donovan—After months of peculiar behavior, Sarah's father is found dead. Did someone get so tired of his questions that they closed his mouth forever?

Bellows—A thug out to take every last penny he can no matter who he destroys along the way. Is he the worst of Sarah's and Nate's problems...or the least?

Mayor Bliss—A rich man elected as mayor year after year. Is there a hidden agenda behind his politics, or are his convictions rock-solid?

Stewart Netters—The editor of the local paper hates Mike Donovan. Was there anything he wouldn't do to keep the man quiet?

Morris Denton—The leader of a group dedicated to empowering teenage males. Is he strengthening or corrupting the morals and ethics of his young charges?

Jason Netters—Nate has a bad feeling the son of the newspaper editor is in over his head. How deeply is he involved in terrorist actions both past and present, and how far will he go to dig himself out?

Alex Foster—Nate's best friend. He was supposed to arrive via his own plane for a rendezvous with Mike and Nate. His plane is late and no one can locate him. Where is he?

Chapter One

After giving the congested waiting area a once-over, Nate Matthews approached the flight center of the tiny Shatterhorn, Nevada, airport with his customary long stride. After hours behind the wheel, it felt good to finally move around. A woman standing behind the counter cast him an anxious smile as she looked up from her computer. He guessed the lousy February weather was playing havoc with things like schedules.

"I'm running a little late," he explained, "and I'm supposed to meet some friends here but I don't see them. Can you tell me if they've arrived?"

"In this weather? I doubt it," she said. "No private planes have landed for at least an hour. Let's take a look. What's their name?"

"Jessica and Alex Foster from Blunt Falls, Montana. He's flying his own single-engine Cessna."

She checked the computer screen, then thumbed through a sheaf of papers, leaving for a moment to talk to a man sitting at a desk behind a glass partition. When she returned, she was shaking her head. "There's a record of Mr. Foster filing his flight plan, but none of him landing here. Looks like you arrived first. Really, though, I'm not sure I'd expect him tonight. The weather is deteriorating quickly, especially at higher elevations."

Nate leaned against the counter for a second. The drive had not been without mishap; in fact, he'd barely survived a blown-out tire and the near collision that followed it. And then he'd found the spare was flat, too. Arranging a tow truck to haul him back to Vegas to get the tire fixed had eaten up time. Alex and Jessica should have landed way ahead of the storm.

The man behind him cleared his throat impatiently and Nate moved away from the counter. Finding a quiet corner, he called Alex's house just in case something had come up at the last moment. Jessica answered the phone.

"Hey," he said after identifying himself. "Is everything there okay?"

"Sure," she said, but her voice sounded stressed. "Is Alex with you?"

"No, that's why I'm calling. Did he leave on time?"

"Yes. He should have been there by now."

"I thought you were coming, too."

"I didn't feel well," she said after a brief hesitation.

He took a deep breath. "I don't mean to alarm you, but I hear there's a storm in the mountains."

"Maybe he had to land somewhere else," she said.

"Maybe. Wouldn't he call you?"

"Not necessarily." There was the edge again. "Anyway, if anything can go wrong with phone service or the radio, you can bet it will. All his equipment is ancient."

Nate stared at the snow falling outside the window. "I'll alert them here. I think you should do the same on your end, just to be safe."

"I will," she said. "But he'll show up. He always does. What would the Blunt Falls police department do without him?"

"Yeah," Nate said, certain now that something was going on with Jessica. His immediate concern, however, was Alex, though he didn't have the slightest idea what he could do about it.

He and Alex had made plans to meet at the airport and then hook up with a third man, a guy by the name of Mike Donovan. They'd only met Mike once, but it had been on a Labor Day afternoon none of the men would ever forget. Alex had told him that this time Jessica was coming along for the ride and maybe a side trip down to Reno.

Nate asked the airport to notify the right people about Alex's flight, tried Mike's cell phone and walked back to his truck through growing snow flurries. Chances were good Mike was sitting at the mall, too distracted to even hear his phone.

He'd been that way lately, posting long emails full of conspiracy theories. Being a deputy in a small town in Arizona, Nate was no stranger to people losing their grip on reality. He just hoped Mike wasn't suffering some sort of post-traumatic stress disorder. Nate himself had struggled coming to grips with what he'd experienced that late summer day, and he'd been in law enforcement his entire adult life. Mike had spent his career either working on the family horse ranch or selling appliances in town.

Even driving up to the cluster of pale stone buildings that constituted the Shatterhorn Mall brought back a hundred unbearable memories for Nate. Last time he'd been here, he and Alex had been returning from an Alaskan fishing trip. When Nate's flight was delayed, the two men had hiked down the road a bit, winding up at this mall, where they found dinner in the food court.

Just an idle diversion to eat up some time on a Labor Day weekend when the place was crammed with kids buying back-to-school clothes. Nate's plan had been to return to the airport in a couple of hours and continue on to Reno and, from there, home. Meanwhile, Alex would fly the Cessna, which he'd left at the airfield ten days before, back to Montana.

Things hadn't exactly turned out as planned.

Today, entering the mall through the doors closest to the food court put a knot in Nate's stomach that twisted tighter with each footstep. It wasn't a big mall by urban standards, but for a small town, it was busy. That was probably why the carnage that had occurred here had upset the nation; this wasn't the kind of town that was supposed to suffer random shootings and mangled teenagers.

Then again, what town was?

The food court was a grand name for ten or eleven fast-food outlets grouped around a few dozen tables. The clientele seemed oblivious to the devastation that had once littered the space. The shattered windows had all been replaced, the bullet holes mended, torn flesh healed or buried… Life went on.

For a moment, Nate stood there, buffeted by the acoustics created by the dome overhead, scanning faces for Mike's, then he turned to leave. As he did so, he caught a glimpse of a familiar face, but it wasn't Mike's.

Jason Netters stood fifteen feet away, very close to the cookie kiosk that came complete with a boatload of tortured memories. Nate had herded a group of kids to the shelter of that kiosk and told them to stay put while he went to help another child. The kids had panicked and left the shelter. The two girls hadn't made it far before being shot and killed, just like two other kids a short distance away.

Jason had survived.

The boy was compact in size but muscular like a wrestler. He had straw-colored hair and green eyes. He must have felt Nate looking at him. Their gazes met and it was as if the past five and a half months had never happened.

The knot grew so tight it was hard to breathe, but Nate took a step forward, unexpectedly moved to see the boy again.

Jason looked away almost at once. Within seconds, he'd disappeared, swallowed up by the crowd, and gone in less time than it took to say it. But the look on his face before he turned unsettled Nate in a way nothing else had.

The boy didn't want to see him. No way. Not one bit.

Nate understood in a moment of clarity that this was the real reason he'd come back here. Not because he believed Mike had earth-shattering news but because this place had cost him a whole lot that September day. He'd walked in one man and left as another, something his fiancée had been quick to point out right before she left for good.

It was come here and face his demons or change careers, because you couldn't be a decent officer when you woke up in a dead sweat every night. His boss was pressing him to run for sheriff in the coming election, said he'd win in a landslide because of the positive light the mall shooting had focused on him. Confused, disgruntled and undecided, he'd taken a leave, parked his career at the door, so to say, while he figured out what the rest of his life looked like. Right now, it was just a blur.

As just about anything was better than spending another minute in this mall, he decided to go find Mike. At least it would put a little distance between himself and the past…for a while, anyway.

HIS ACTUAL DESTINATION, programmed into the truck's on-board GPS, was thirty miles west of Reno. He knew Mike lived on a horse ranch he'd inherited from his father and that he was divorced, with one daughter from whom it seemed he was estranged. Nate wasn't sure where the daughter was now. Boston or New York or maybe Washington, D.C., somewhere on the East Coast. He'd read a brief account of Mike's family in the newspaper after the shooting.

Thanks to a cold, brisk wind, the driving was tricky, but the roads were mercifully clear of snow and ice, at least at first. Too preoccupied to take note of the scenery, even if he'd been able to see it through the weather and darkness, he traveled in a cocoon of steel, falling into an odd trancelike state where he could have been anyone going anywhere. He kind of wanted to keep driving forever.

After thirty minutes, the directions had him turn off the highway and drive uphill over another ten miles of increasingly untended roads. Maybe the reason Mike hadn't shown was as simple as Alex's—the storm and the inclement weather had prohibited travel. Nate had snow tires on his vehicle, chains in the back and nowhere else to go, nothing else to do, so he kept driving.

He finally came across a sign hanging from a frame by one rusted chain. He emerged from the truck to find the snow deeper here. He'd get stuck if he wasn't careful. Picking his way forward, he tilted the dangling sign toward his headlights and read, "Donovan's Fine Quarter Horses Since 1936."

The place had obviously seen better days, as was increasingly evident as he drove the remaining distance up the overgrown road. He broke out into a clearing upon which sat numerous outbuildings and what appeared to be empty pastures, though he could hear the noise of a horse somewhere nearby. The house itself was dark and looked abandoned. Nate pulled his vehicle to a stop beside an older truck that could have been sitting there an hour or five years. It was quickly being buried in the snow, which was falling fast now. He had no idea what Mike drove. He gritted his teeth as he dug a flashlight out of his glove box.

Had Mike succumbed to the weather or was it more

serious, something like a heart attack or a stroke? Was he inside that house, dead or dying? That would explain why he hadn't answered any of Nate's calls.

Nate flashed his light over the broken pavers that jutted out of the snow. He stumbled over a planter that had frozen and shattered, spilling its contents sometime in the past. He recovered without falling, catching himself by grabbing a porch rail that wobbled when he grasped it. As he flicked the light over the door, shivers that had nothing to do with the temperature raced down his spine and across his back. The door was ajar but he could see no glint of light through the opening.

Since Sept. 11, police officers were allowed to carry weapons across state lines, but Nate had left his behind with his badge. In his head, the two went together. But now, unarmed, he felt naked, a sensation that echoed the way he'd felt months before when hell broke loose in the mall. Now, he swore to himself, come hell or high water, he would never step foot in Nevada again without a gun.

With the flashlight, he nudged the door open quietly, relieved when it didn't creak or groan. He flashed the light around and took in a large entry with three connecting doorways that seemed to lead to a dining area, living room and hallway.

He tried a light switch and was surprised when it worked. He thought he heard a sound from somewhere deep in the house, but at that second, in the improved light, he caught a glimpse of something that focused all his attention ahead.

A body lay sprawled facedown on the floor right inside the living room. Nate gasped a shallow breath. This sure explained why Mike was late.

Chapter Two

Nate knelt beside the body and rolled it over, knowing who and what he would find when he did so. Or at least he'd thought he knew. The who was easy. Mike was dead. The what was a shock.

Not a heart attack, not a stroke, but a massive gunshot wound to the chest had ended Mike's life. His clothes were soaked in blood, his pale eyes half-open, his lidded gaze fixed and empty. Nate had run across more than his share of shooting victims, and now he scanned the area for some sign of the weapon that had caused this catastrophic damage. He felt for a pulse, knowing he wouldn't find one, and did his best to block out the smell of blood. He quickly searched Mike's pockets for a phone or anything else that might help explain what had happened before he died. He found nothing.

He sat back on his heels. Poor Mike, poor guy. To survive the mall, to actually be the one to wrestle the wounded killer to the ground and hear his dying words, only to end up like this five and a half months later in his own home…

There was that noise again. Was the killer still in the house? From the look of things, an intruder had walked right in and caught Mike coming from the living room. He wore an unzipped jacket, as though he'd been in the process of leaving the house. The room had the appearance of having been searched, and none too carefully, either.

The house was cold, no lights, no fire in the grate, impossible to tell how long ago this had happened. There was no smell of gunpowder in the room, but with an open door that didn't really mean much.

He listened carefully as he stood up, once again scanning for something with which to arm himself. All he could see was a fireplace poker, and that struck him as pretty low-tech when it came to confronting whatever had taken down Mike. On the other hand, it was better than nothing. He crossed the room silently, snatched the poker from atop the hearth and stood stock-still, listening.

Another noise, like a door closing. He followed it across the living room and into the entry. He was certain it came from down the hall. He had a quick look at the kitchen and the laundry room, noting the disarray of cupboards and drawers. What in the heck had someone looked for—and had they found it?

The outside door was locked. He turned around and retraced his steps, switching on lights as he moved. Whoever was here must have heard him rustling around, probably seen the lights come on. There was no possibility to surprise them.

A more prudent plan of action would be to head for the relative safety of his truck and call the police, but then the intruder might escape through a back window or destroy evidence. All but holding his breath, Nate nudged open the first door on his left.

From the threshold, he could see the room held a lone twin bed and nightstand, a small chest of drawers and a few boxes stacked in the corner. The closet doors were folded open and the overhead lamp revealed three hangers. There were a couple of empty cardboard boxes inside the closet, their contents heaped beside them. Ditto the boxes in the corner. The drawers were all open.

The door across the hall led to another small room furnished with a futon, a small television and a desk piled high with papers and books. The drawers in this room were open as well, the items they'd apparently once held now scattered across the floor. It looked as though a computer used to occupy the desktop, but all that was left now was a mouse and a few cords. He checked the closet, but it was empty. He found the main bathroom in a similar state of disrepair and pulled the shower curtain back to make sure no one was hiding there.

The last door opened onto what was obviously Mike's bedroom. It held an unmade queen-size bed, a dresser and a couple of chairs. Piles of clothing littered every horizontal surface and the air smelled stale and unused, but it didn't appear to have been ransacked like the rest of the house. The bathroom off of this room was empty. That left the closet.

Wait just a second. Surely the person who had gunned down Mike in cold blood wasn't now cowering in a closet? Well, it was either that or they'd found a way around to the front of the house or out a window.

Holding the poker high, Nate planted his feet firmly, stood off to one side and yanked open the door. At first he saw nothing but the usual array of hanging clothes and a locked gun cabinet. Then he saw the clothes rustle. Peering into a gloomy jumble of boots on the floor, he glimpsed two smaller shoes. One moved slightly. Someone was hiding in here.

"Come on out," he demanded, his grip tightening on the poker.

"Don't shoot," a shaky voice responded.

Using his free hand, Nate pushed back the clothes and

found a woman scrunched as far back into the closet as was humanly possible. It was so dark back there that she was little more than glistening eyes and a pale oval for a face.

"I'm not going to shoot," he said, resisting the urge to shine the flashlight on her.

"Why did you kill my dad?" she asked, and he could hear the effort it took for her to spit out these words. "What good is that going to do?"

"You're Mike's daughter?"

She caught a new sob in her throat and wiped at her eyes. Even in the dim light, he could see her fingers shake as they grazed her cheek. "I...I was," she said.

He offered her a hand because she appeared ready to keel over. "I didn't kill Mike, but it sounds like you know who did. Please, come out of there. Did you see or hear anyone?"

"No," she said. "Nothing."

"Come on," he coaxed, touching her shoulder. "I'm not going to hurt you. My name is Nate Matthews. I was a friend of your dad's."

"From the store? He quit, you know. He couldn't concentrate on selling things anymore. He said... Well, never mind."

"No, I didn't know he quit his job. I didn't work with him. I'm from down in Arizona."

"Oh, my God," she said, her hands flying to her mouth. "You're one of the men who was at the mall last summer with Dad. You're the deputy sheriff."

"Yeah," he said without correcting her.

She seemed to relax a tiny bit and allowed him to help her from the shadows of the closet.

Seen in brighter light, she turned out to be a little older than his first estimate of late teens, and he adjusted her age to mid-twenties, a decade or so younger than him. She had a very pale complexion, her flawless cheeks moist from tears. A sheath of black hair caught the light and reflected it, setting off the bluest eyes Nate had ever seen. She was tall, probably five-seven or so, with full breasts and a small waist, attributes her black turtleneck sweater clearly revealed. Tight jeans announced the other half of her was just as fit. A pair of worn equestrian boots hugged her calves.

Her eyes grew huge as he pulled his phone from a pocket. "What are you doing?" she demanded, catching his hand.

"Calling the police."

"No! You mustn't. Please."

"Listen…" He paused, not knowing her name.

"Sarah. Sarah Donovan."

"Sarah, if there is one thing I'm absolutely positive I must do, it's call the police. This is not open for debate." But why wouldn't she want him to call for help? For that matter, why hadn't she? "When did this happen?" he added when he found he had no signal.

She was studying her watch, and whatever she found there seemed to alarm her. She looked up as though she'd only half heard him. "What? The shooting? I'm not sure when it happened. I just got here a little while ago."

"From where?"

She hesitated a moment before saying, "What's it to you?"

"How did you get here?"

"I flew."

His brow furrowed.

"I landed in Reno and rented a car. It's out in the barn. Why are you looking at me like that?"

He ignored her question. "Does your dad have a phone?"

"He got rid of the landline, but he has a cell."

"I checked his body. He's not carrying it."

"He always carries it," she insisted.

He frowned at her again. "Do you have any ID?"

"What!"

"Look at it from my point of view. You're the only person in the house with a dead man and I'm supposed to take it at face value that you are who you say you are? For that matter, put up your hands. I'm going to frisk you."

"Why?"

"Because Mike was shot in the chest and I don't want the same thing to happen to me. Put up your hands."

"Or you'll what? Hit me with a fire poker? Really?"

"Really," he said, his tone serious.

She glowered at him as she raised her hands. He patted her down with one hand while still clutching the poker with the other.

"Satisfied?" she said when he was finished.

"You could have hidden a weapon somewhere in the house. What about some ID?"

"I left it in the car."

"Why would you do that?"

"I wasn't planning on being here very long."

"So, you flew here all the way from who knows where, parked in an old barn, came into a dark house—"

"It wasn't dark when I got here," she interrupted. "After I saw my dad lying on the floor, I heard an engine and thought his killer had come back, so I turned off the lights and hid. It must have been you."

"Do you have any idea why the house was searched?"

Her gaze flicked to the floor and back. "No."

He stared at her a moment. "Let's go get your ID."

"I have a better idea. Why don't you drive back into

town where your phone gets reception and summon the cops? I'll stay here. With Dad."

"You'll stay here," he said, his voice very dry.

"Yes. Now what's wrong?"

"I still don't know who you are. I'm not leaving you alone in this house."

She rubbed her forehead as though she was so frustrated with him she had to fight to maintain control.

"Let's go get your ID," he repeated.

She didn't look happy about the prospect, but when he started to touch her arm, she drew away and took off down the hall. He stayed close behind her, telling himself not to get distracted by the way her hips moved inside the black denim.

"I need my coat," she said, gesturing at the chair behind Mike's body. As she spoke, her gaze traveled down to her father's still form and she caught a sob in her throat. She flicked away new tears as Nate handed her the coat. He did his best to look away for a moment.

When she finally spoke again, her voice was a little shaky. She'd zipped a dark blue down parka up to her chin. The color emphasized the sapphire hue of her eyes. "I just wish I'd known him better," she whispered.

Nate felt the same way, but wasn't it odd that Mike's daughter did, as well? Maybe Mike wasn't the easiest guy to get to know.

Sarah turned suddenly and met his gaze. "I'll go get my purse," she said. "No reason for us both to freeze to death."

"I don't mind," he said.

"Which really means you don't trust me."

He shrugged one shoulder. "Shall we?"

"Like I have a choice." Once again she glanced at her watch, this time emitting a small gasp. It gave him the willies. Why was she worried about time? Was she waiting for an accomplice to show up?

He followed her out the front door, amazed how much more snow had accumulated in the few minutes he'd been inside. His own white truck was covered with the stuff, as was the other. The wind had also picked up, blowing icy crystals at their faces as they started across the yard. He held the Stetson on his head and was glad he'd worn his trusty cowboy boots.

"I left the car in that barn over there," she said. She opened the sliding door a couple of feet and they walked inside. Nate flicked on his flashlight as he heard a horse whinny nearby.

"That's Skipjack," she said. "He's the last horse Dad has. Had."

Nate nodded, but his concentration was really on the old green sedan sitting ten feet in front of them. "You rented *that* at an airport?" he asked.

"Sort of," she said.

"What's that mean?"

"It means I rented it from a place that specializes in wrecks. It wasn't exactly at the airport."

"Good grief," he said.

"My purse is in the backseat on the left by my suitcase. It's unlocked."

He moved around the car to the far side. Opening the back door, he shined the light into the interior. "I don't see anything—" he began, glancing up, and for a second, he wasn't sure what had happened. The woman was gone as if she'd never existed. Then reason took hold— she must have run out the door while he was distracted. Swearing, he raced around the car and shined his light across the yard in time to see the driver's door of his truck slam closed.

As he followed the path she'd plowed through the snow, he heard the automatic click of his door lock. He shined the light at the driver's window and saw her searching everywhere for something. She finally turned on the cab light and lowered the visor, patting it as though she thought a key might be lurking up there. He saw her cup her forehead with one hand, wincing in defeat. Her lips moved as if she swore. Then she looked at him through the foggy glass.

Taking the ring of keys out of his pocket, he dangled them in front of his side of the tinted window. Her eyes narrowed and her lips moved again. This time he was sure she swore. He pressed the automatic lock button and opened the door.

"Who in the hell are you?" he asked her.

"Just who I said I was. Sarah Donovan."

"Why are you acting so peculiar?"

"I have to get out of here. Now."

"Why?"

"It's none of your business," she said with a pleading note in her voice.

"Well, actually, grand theft auto is my business when it's my damn truck. Did you kill Mike?"

"No, of course not. Everything happened just the way I said."

"Why can't I quite believe that?" he mused aloud, offering her a hand down.

She ignored his help and jumped to the ground, where she slipped on the compacted snow and started to fall. He caught her shoulders and she looked up at him. "You can't believe me because you're cynical," she said. "Every cop I've ever known gets to be like that."

"And have you known a lot of cops?"

"My share," she said. "I even married one a long time ago. Listen, please, just let me leave."

"The police will want to talk to you," he said, letting her go.

"So, I'll come back."

Sure she would. He shook his head. "Sorry."

"Is your phone working? Could I at least make a call?"

He dug his phone out of his jacket pocket. Maybe he could get a signal outside. The screen lit up with a swipe of his finger, and in that instant, a loud pop cracked the frigid air. His phone blew out of his hand and disintegrated into nothing. He grabbed his throbbing fingers with his free hand, dropping the flashlight in the process. Another shot came next and he actually felt the bullet whiz past his left ear. Without thinking, he grabbed Sarah and pulled her to the ground. The flashlight had landed a couple of feet away and sank into the fresh snow, where it now illuminated a small crater and pinpointed their location as clear as day.

"Are you hurt?" he whispered to Sarah.

"No," she murmured. "Are you?"

His hand throbbed. "I'll live. We have to move."

"Your truck..."

"We'd be sitting ducks. The snow's too deep and we can't dig it out with a gunman taking shots at us."

"Then my car."

Another bullet came dangerously close. "Do you want to race across the yard in this snow with someone shooting at you? Besides, your rent-a-wreck is so low to the ground you couldn't drive through the snow even if we did manage to get it out of the barn."

As though privy to their conversation, a couple more shots and a nearby popping sound announced at least one of the truck tires had just bitten the dust.

"Then where?" she said.

"Back to the house. Stay in the shadows and stick close. Ready?"

He wasn't positive, but he thought he detected a slight nod.

Chapter Three

Sarah's head was filled with so many images and worries that for an instant, she almost couldn't bring herself to move. What in the world was she going to do? A bullet hit the snow a couple of feet from her hand and that cleared her mind, at least for the moment. First things first.

She scrambled to follow in Nate's wake, doing her best to keep her head and butt down. If this gunman was who she thought he was, he wouldn't be firing to kill them but to capture them and force information. There would be no quick, clean death, not for her, anyway. The thought of torture created a layer of sweat on top of her icy skin.

She hadn't known who or what to expect when the closet door opened, but it sure as heck hadn't been a tall glowering cowboy, although now that she stopped to think, she should have realized he'd come. How would she get rid of him?

She'd read about Nate Matthews after the Labor Day shooting. She knew he was engaged, that he was respected down in Arizona and that he didn't tolerate any nonsense. She knew his service record and the fact his parents had been photographed looking as proud as peacocks about their upstanding son. And she knew her father had trusted him and his friend Alex. Maybe they'd been the only people her father had trusted toward the end. She sure didn't have a place on that short list.

Hopefully, Nate Matthews would figure out how to get out of this situation and go for help. That would give her the opportunity to finish what she'd started and try to escape.

There was a sincerity in his eyes that made her uneasy about this possibility, but it was clear he didn't believe much of what she said, and that was good. Sooner or later, if they weren't shot first, he'd grow weary of her behavior and cut his losses. All she had to do was wait him out.

Except that took time and time was something she had precious little of. And face it, she was whisper close to being his adversary, or at least he would see it that way, and he didn't appear to be the kind of man you wanted to be on the bad side of. If he'd just let her leave when she'd tried to, then she'd be on her way back to Reno and none of this would have happened.

You'd be on your way empty-handed, her racing mind reminded her, *driving a stolen truck with this killer on your heels. And don't forget, empty-handed means by this time tomorrow, you'll be an orphan.*

"You still with me?" Nate hissed when he paused behind a row of arborvitae. A shot went off, but it hit several feet to their left, over by a planter that would be filled with wildflowers in three months if it survived the night.

"I'm here," she whispered, bumping into him as she scooted to pull her foot into the shadow.

"Listen," he said, his voice very soft, his lips right next to her ear. He'd grabbed her shoulder with one hand when she'd tumbled against him and he didn't release it now. His strong grip was oddly reassuring and his warm breath against her frozen ear distracted her for a second. "I'm concerned this could be a trap."

"What do you mean?"

"There could be another gunman waiting inside the house."

A serious shiver ran up both her arms, made a U-turn and raced right back down to her fingertips. That was exactly what Bellows would plan—a trap where she'd be forced to spill her guts. But how did you spill your guts about something you didn't know anything about?

"The back door is locked," he added, as if to himself.

"Not if you know where the key is."

"And you do?"

"I think so," she said, hoping it was still where her father used to keep it. She hadn't lived in this house for eleven years. By now the key could be lost, the lock might have been changed... Who knew? "There's a fake brick next to the steps."

"Let's go," he said as he tossed a rock several feet across to the other side of the porch. It hit a drainpipe or something else metallic. A round of deafening shots galvanized her as Nate grabbed her hand and tugged her in the other direction, around the corner of the house. From the sound of things, Nate's truck had just lost a window and a couple more tires, or maybe the shots had hit her father's old beater.

They crawled behind the row of camellias her mother had planted in the far past. The snow was deep, but not as deep as in the yard itself, thanks to the bushes and the overhanging eaves. As a child, she'd had to be bribed to come back here to turn on the water or hook up a hose because of the spiders that lurked in the leafy darkness. Tonight, spiders seemed like a distant threat from more innocent days.

"It should be right around here," she said as they scooted into a small clearing by the back porch. The snow covered almost everything and they both dug like harried rabbits. "I got it," she said, her voice raw from the cold. She picked up a brick that appeared slightly smaller than the others. Her fingers were so numb she couldn't discern the texture of the stone, but it felt blessedly light, as though it wasn't really made out of clay. She wiggled the bottom and a panel slid open to reveal something that twinkled in the indirect light seeping through the window above.

"Eureka," Nate whispered as she shook the key out into his hand. She remained crouched while he slowly got to his feet. A second later, she heard the sound of the key in the lock. "You stay here. I'll go check," he said, his face surrounded by a veil of condensed breath.

She didn't respond, just followed behind him through the back door, closing it quietly behind her, ignoring his disgruntled expression when he turned around and found her standing there. No way was she staying outside alone. Besides, it was at least a little warmer in here and she was frozen to the bone.

"Did your father own a gun?" he whispered.

"He used to. If he still has it, it would be in that locked cabinet in the back of his closet."

"And the key?"

"I didn't have time to look for it." Truth was, she'd been searching for that key when she'd heard Nate arrive.

"I'll find it," Nate said. He stared down at her, his features visible for the first time in what seemed a long time. His skin was slightly tanned, as though he spent a fair amount of time outdoors. His hair was long for a lawman, thick and dark, his lashes luxuriant, his gray eyes wary. She hadn't noticed his dark eyebrows before, how straight they were and how they framed his eyes. They currently furled inward as he studied her. "Can I trust you to stay by this door and yell like a banshee if anyone approaches it?"

"You mean as opposed to running outside and taking my chances with a gun?" His eyes narrowed now and she could sense the lingering distrust. "Sorry," she said, relenting. "Okay, I'll act as lookout. Just hurry."

He nodded once, quick and decisive. Arming himself with a knife from the metallic strip mounted above the cooktop, he left the kitchen and headed toward the entry hall without making a sound, although he did leave a trail of dirty melting snow behind him.

The knife struck her as an excellent idea, so she grabbed one for herself and slid the deadbolt closed. This time when she glanced at her watch, her heart all but stopped beating. The night was being gobbled up like Christmas dinner and she felt like the main course. For a second she considered dimming the lights, but thought better of it. She could still hear the occasional shot coming from the yard and figured the gunman must be shooting at shadows. No need to alert him the game had moved indoors.

How could she even joke about this being a game? Her dad was dead and it might very well be her fault, no matter how unreasonable he'd been. If she didn't get real clever or real lucky very soon, then her mother would pay the price as well. Nope, this wasn't a game.

A flash of light out in the yard, barely visible now because of the falling snow, caught her attention and she involuntarily jerked. The window in the door exploded and she hit the floor along with a shower of safety glass. Yelling like crazy, she scrambled to her feet and dashed toward the front hall, sure the gunman was seconds away from crashing through the door.

She ran right into Nate, who had managed to find a rifle. He immediately caught her around the waist and swung her behind him, then continued on into the kitchen while she clung to the faux paneling, the knife gripped in her white-knuckled hand. Her gaze followed him as he ran to the door and started firing shots through the broken window.

He knelt to reload, his concentration so intent on the gun and the ammunition that he might have been in a different world. He stood again and aimed, letting off a few rounds, then waited. It had grown ominously quiet outside.

Up until that point, Sarah had thought of Nate as part obstacle and part protector, a leader, but standing there, his jeans wet from melting snow, his taut body ready for action, he came into sharper focus as a fellow human being who had walked into a mess not of his own making and was now stuck.

She lowered her gaze. She knew he would do everything in his power to safeguard her, whether he trusted her or not. That should have reassured her. Instead, along with everything else, it made her stomach roll.

After several very long moments, he turned to look at her and their gazes connected like two hot wires with a spark in the middle. She drew a small, quick breath, surprised by the tension between them that suddenly leaped with awareness. It was almost as if he could read her mind and knew darn well that she was determined to leave this ranch as soon as she could.

"You look scared," he whispered.

"And you're not?"

"Nerves of steel," he said, but he said it with a self-deprecating smile and a soft shake of his head.

"There's nobody else in the house?" she asked.

"Nope, we're alone."

She gestured with her head toward the broken window and the seeming emptiness of the backyard. "Do you think you hit him?"

"Either that or he's circling around to the front."

Sarah turned her head suddenly. "What's that sound?"

He cocked his head and listened for a second, then strode toward her. "That's a two-stroke engine," he said. They both raced into the entry, where it was obvious the noise came from outside the house. They flanked the door and peered through the small inset piece of glass. At first there was nothing to see, then a light blazed on, wavering through the snow. "Headlight," Nate said under his breath.

Sarah looked up at him. "Just one?"

"A damn snowmobile," he said, lifting the rifle. "I should have guessed. How else would anyone get up here and away again? Okay, stay put, and this time I mean it!" He was out the front door and headed into the storm before Sarah could even react to his madness. Wrapping her arms around herself, she turned into the room and recoiled as her father's bloody body met her gaze.

There was nothing she could do to help him—or Nate, either, for that matter. What she did have was an unforeseen few moments alone to try to finish what she'd come for. Otherwise, in less than twenty-four hours, her mother would be dead. Sarah desperately needed to pull a rabbit out of a hat.

No, that wasn't true. She needed two rabbits.

All she had to do was find two hats. And the only place she could think to look that she hadn't already was the safe.

KEEPING TO THE SHADOWS and wishing like crazy he had a flashlight, Nate skirted the yard. The snow was falling so fast and furious it was hard to get his bearings. He could no longer see the dim house lights or a vehicle headlight, either, but he could hear the engine and so far it didn't appear to be moving away. He just tried to follow the sound, but the wind roaring through the overhead branches made even that chore tricky.

Armed only with Mike's six-shot Winchester saddle gun that was undoubtedly older than he was, Nate's impromptu plan included tackling the gunman and subduing him. The bonus would be gaining control of the snowmobile, which could then be used to get to a place where they could summon help. Because it was obvious there was no way the truck could be fixed and driven in this weather. And that car of Sarah's was a joke.

He wasn't going to allow himself to think about Sarah and all the ways she confused him, at least not right now. There was something strange about her, but he needed to focus his attention on the matter at hand.

The engine pitch changed, and he knew his quarry was about to leave. The snow was too deep for him to run, but he slogged through as fast as he could, his plan seeming more naive by the moment. By luck, he bumped into what felt like a pile of rocks, and that at last gave him some semifirm footing. Using his numb hands and clutching the rifle with a death grip, he scrambled up on top in time to see the vehicle's headlight passing to his left. He fired off a few shots, knowing this was a last hurrah, then threw caution to the wind and leaped toward the lights, reaching out to grab where he assumed the driver would be seated.

A sudden burning sensation flared in his left arm. His fingers brushed hot metal for a microsecond before he found himself facedown in the snow with a mouth full of exhaust. He still grasped the rifle and was kind of amazed he hadn't shot himself, though his arm throbbed. As he sat up, the roar of the snowmobile sounded like evil laughter. The taillights had already disappeared. By the time he got to his feet, even the motor sound had been swallowed up by the night.

The gunman was gone.

He clutched his left biceps and wasn't surprised when

his hand came away bloody. He hadn't wounded himself with his own rifle, but the gunman must have gotten off a parting shot.

So much for leaving the gun and badge back in Arizona. If he'd come armed with a decent weapon, this could all be over now, and once again, the inadequate feelings from being helpless during the mall shooting all but choked him. Why had he thought he could run away from being who he was?

He had to get back to the house, and that meant figuring out which way it lay, then getting there before hypothermia set in. This time when he questioned Sarah, she'd better say something worth listening to.

Chapter Four

By the time Nate finally bumped into his truck and stumbled the rest of the way to the house, he was experiencing an eerie sensation of being frozen and light-headed at the same time. His trusty jacket was more or less toast, but it had probably saved his life by maintaining his core temperature. Good thing he'd never had the opportunity to take it off.

He had no idea where or when he'd lost his hat, and his head was freezing. He loved the old Stetson, but hats came and went just like women.

All this was flittering through his mind while his light flashed over his truck, and he swore. He'd just finished paying the blasted thing off and he was no longer on the receiving end of a monthly paycheck. Look at the poor thing. The windshield had somehow survived, but the passenger window was gone, half the tires blown out, bullet holes down one side, and that was just what he could see in a glance. He swore again and felt like kicking something.

By the time he got inside the house, he was cold from temperature and anger. First thing to take care of was his arm. Hopefully he wouldn't need to depend on Sarah to help him—so far she hadn't struck him as the helpful type.

Where was she, anyway? Why hadn't she been waiting at the door, anxious to hear the outcome of his mission? What was more important to her than staying alive?

Bypassing Mike's body, he grabbed a bright throw from the back of a chair and started to drape it across the dead man, then stopped. The least he could do was preserve the crime scene until the experts got here. The camera on his phone had exploded with everything else, but maybe he'd find another one somewhere in with Mike's possessions.

Which reminded him that Mike's keys, wallet and cell appeared to be missing, along with his computer and who knew what else. Was this a robbery gone wrong or was it something more complicated?

He dropped the throw back on the chair and went looking for Sarah. He found her in her father's room, poking into the now unlocked gun cabinet that Nate had opened by finding the key tucked away in the pocket of the hunting vest hanging beside it.

"What are you doing?" he said.

She turned suddenly, a bulging manila envelope in her hands. There were additional boxes and envelopes piled on the bed as well. Her eyes widened as though she'd forgotten he was there. Or maybe she was just startled he'd made it back alive. "Did you get him?" she asked. "Did you see who it was?"

"No to both," he said.

She swallowed as she pushed her left hand down into her pocket. Was she holding something? The past hour or so had somehow honed her beauty into a grittier, darker form, enhanced by the dirt smudged on her jeans and across her cheek. In all honesty, it made her twice as sexy as she'd been, and that was saying something.

His head swam in the sudden heat of the room and he swayed a little. "What's in the envelope?"

"Dad's retirement stuff. I was looking for some old papers of mine."

"Old papers," he responded, his voice dry.

"Yeah. School papers, my diploma… Listen, it doesn't matter. They're not here."

"Anything else interesting in there?" he asked, nodding toward the safe.

"No," she said quickly. "Just genealogy stuff. Dad got off on that tangent a few years ago when he and Mom split up." She stared harder at him, then gasped. "You're bleeding!"

He followed the direction of her gaze to the torn, blood-soaked sleeve of his jacket and the red smears on his hand. "Yeah," he said and sat down abruptly on the side of the bed.

She was there in front of him almost at once. "What happened?"

"Score one for the bad guy."

"Oh, man, this is my fault," she said, running to the adjoining bathroom and returning with a stack of clean towels. "Take off your jacket. Here, I'll help you."

She very carefully unzipped the front of his jacket, which put her head next to his, and he breathed in the scents of hay and snow, an odd combination and bracingly refreshing. Her hair brushed his forehead and he closed his eyes, not trusting himself to look at her. He'd always been a sucker for blue eyes and this wasn't the time or place for that kind of thing.

"Easy now," she coaxed and gingerly helped him get his good arm out of the sleeve. Then she began peeling away the other sleeve, which hurt like blazes, and he winced.

"Sorry," she said. "Almost done." She dropped the jacket to the floor. "We'd better get your shirt off, too." That took longer and was agonizing for Nate as she freed his good arm from the heather-gray Henley and began the painstaking process of loosening the other sleeve from his injured arm.

"It's stuck to the blood," she explained.

He swallowed and nodded.

"Just a minute, okay?" She went back to the bathroom and returned a moment later with a brown bottle of hydrogen peroxide and bandages. "Maybe this will help," she said and, using the towel beneath his arm to absorb the overflow, drenched the site with the peroxide, loosening the knitted material from the wound. A moment later she managed to slip the shirt over his head and he sighed deeply with profound relief.

She looked a little pale as she considered his arm but, to her credit, didn't shy away. Instead she used more of the peroxide to bathe the site and peered intently at it.

Nate turned his head to try to get a good look. He was way too aware of her hand resting atop his bare shoulder, her fingers trembling as though her external coolness masked an inner repulsion at the sight of bloody flesh. The tip of her tongue flicked across her lips and he took a deep breath. He wasn't sure if his reactions to her proximity were an attempt to distance himself from his injury or because he'd have to be in far worse shape than he was *not* to notice her.

"I think the bullet entered and exited the fleshy part of your arm," she said.

He flexed his hand and tried out a smile. "It must not have hit anything too important on its way. It looks more like a graze to me. More of a nuisance than a danger."

"Spoken like a true he-man."

"Spoken like a guy stuck in the middle of a shoot-out."

"I'll wrap it with gauze."

A few intense minutes later, his biceps was bandaged

and she'd found a wool shirt of her dad's with the tags still attached. "I sent him this for Christmas," she said. "I guess he didn't like the color."

The color looked fine to Nate, kind of a deep blue. She guided it gently over his bandaged arm, then insisted on buttoning it for him. Once again, her face was close to his as she performed this chore, and once again, every one of his senses jumped into hyperdrive.

He caught her hand as she straightened up. "I could tell it was an…unpleasant…task for you," he said, running his thumb over the tops of her fingers. "Thanks."

"No big deal," she said. "I've always tended animals, you know. In fact, I wanted to be a veterinarian."

"What happened?"

"Life," she said. "Now I work at animal clinics. Anyway, I've seen my share of bloody messes."

"Still, your hand shook," he said. "Maybe human gore is worse than animal."

She shrugged and looked away. It was obvious to him that she wanted to let matters drop, but he couldn't quite dismiss the feel of her fingers against his skin. Nevertheless, there were more urgent matters at hand. "I assume that old truck parked out front was your father's only vehicle?"

"Yes. Why?"

"Because someone took his keys and wallet."

"His keys." If possible, she went whiter still. "Oh, my gosh. His garage."

"What garage?"

"One of those storage units over in Shatterhorn. Maybe someone wanted access to it. I didn't even think of that."

"What did he keep in it?"

"Who knows? When I was a kid he kept business-related items there. I'm not even sure he still has it."

"Okay, well, try this. Did he ever say anything to you about someone threatening him?"

"Not directly, but I know he's felt restless and out of sorts since Labor Day and the mall shooting. Being the closest in proximity when the shooter killed himself really affected him, especially after the carnage the guy had created. And there was that last word the man spoke, too. It worried Dad."

"You mean *pearl,*" Nate said.

"Yeah."

One of the mall jewelry stores had contracted to keep a pricey shipment of Tahitian black pearls that were in transit to a big casino down in Vegas. The police had voiced the theory that the kid planned to steal them, but it seemed unlikely to Nate. Since when did a nineteen-year-old bring two loaded weapons to a shopping mall on the busiest afternoon of the summer to steal pearls? And if that had been his plan, why kill four people before taking his own life?

"I don't know," Sarah said. "Since the shooter never got around to actually stealing the pearls, Dad worried someone else would step in and try to do it. For a while he drove into town almost every day, watching and waiting. I tried to tell him the pearl shipment had been sent away the very next day, but he didn't believe me, even when I sent him the newspaper article."

"I didn't know he was that troubled," Nate said quietly, but it didn't surprise him. When something horrific happened to a person, they were often driven to try to make sense of it. And sometimes, there just wasn't a way to do that.

"Anyway," she continued, "he'd been questioning everyone, making a nuisance of himself—at least that's what I heard."

"From who?"

"Someone told me."

"Someone reliable?"

"More or less. My, er, source said Dad nagged the newspaper, the mayor, the police—anyone he could get to sit still while he expounded on his theories. I don't think he made a lot of friends lately. And, of course, he knew Thomas Jacks. Everyone knew him."

Thomas Jacks was the name of the gunman. Nate should have realized that in a town the size of Shatterhorn, people were likely to know one another.

"He just couldn't get over the fact that boy caused all that heartache," Sarah continued, "and not to just himself, but to his family. Even his past schoolmates, like Jason Netters. People kept asking themselves if they should have seen this coming, but by all accounts, Thomas was a good kid who loved his family and his country—it just didn't make any sense."

Was that why Jason had survived the barrage of bullets that had killed the two girls who had fled the protection of the cookie kiosk with him? Had Thomas spared his friend, or was it even possible Jason had been part of the crime?

"Did your father know Jason?"

"I don't know. He knew Thomas because I babysat for him and his brother a few times. But Jason's dad, Stewart Netters, is the newspaper editor, so I'm sure he got to know him recently."

"I remember Netters," Nate said. "He interviewed me and your dad and Alex after the shooting."

"I read the article. Mayor Bliss hailed you guys as heroes. He said the whole thing would have been worse if the three of you hadn't kept everyone calm. Dad said he didn't deserve any accolades, that it was you and Mr. Foster who had police experience."

"Your dad underestimated his role," Nate said. The intended compliments she'd passed on about Nate made him cringe inside. He'd lost the lives of the two kids he felt responsible for—he was no hero. Desperate now to get the topic off of that day, he abruptly changed the subject. "Did you happen to find a camera anywhere?"

"It's in the bottom drawer of his dresser," she said. "Why?"

"Precaution," he said, recovering the camera and checking to see if it contained film, which it did. From the corner of his eye he could see Sarah dividing her attention between him and her watch. What had she stuck in her pocket? Would she tell him if he asked? He doubted it, so he didn't ask.

For a few minutes when she'd been helping him, he'd glimpsed a calmer, gentler side of her, but the nervous one was emerging again, complete with quick glances and fidgety hands.

"I need to get out of here," she said under her breath.

"We need to talk," he said.

"I don't have time to talk. I have to get back to Reno."

"Listen, if you won't tell me what's making you so damn anxious to leave in the middle of this storm, will you at least explain why you tried to ditch me and who the heck our visitor was?"

"I don't know who it was," she said with a subtle shift of her gaze that told him she was hedging at best, probably lying.

"Then why did you say my getting shot was your fault?"

"I said that? I don't know."

"You have an idea who this assailant is, don't you?"

"No, none. How could I? Like I said, I hadn't seen Dad in a while."

"Then why did you come here?"

"I just wanted to talk to him."

"About what?"

"How is that any of your business?"

They were back to square one, her defiantly standing her ground, him floundering around in the dark. He shook his head and headed toward the door. "You know, you're a beautiful woman, Sarah Donovan," he said, pausing by her side to look down at her. Big mistake—those eyes looked so innocent and guileless. "Under other circumstances I bet you're fascinating company," he added, "but right now, I'd settle for some straight answers."

"Unfortunately, I have nothing to offer."

"How about ID? Where is your purse or wallet or whatever?"

"It was taken from me. I have no identification with me."

"And yet you managed to rent that bucket of bolts in the barn?"

"My stuff was taken after I rented the car."

"So the rental agreement is in the car?"

"No, it was in my purse."

He took a deep breath.

"Will you try to stop me if I leave?" she asked.

"Unless you can fly, I don't see how you're going to get out of here. But, yes, I *will* stop you." He continued on his way.

For the next few minutes, he busied himself taking pictures of Mike's still form and the surrounding area, covering his friend's hands with plastic bags from the kitchen. He committed to memory any detail that might someday be relevant. While he did all this, he kept an ear out for Sarah, but things had grown very quiet. He was angling a shot from near the fireplace when a photograph propped up on the mantelpiece caught his attention, and he paused to study it.

There was Mike, not too long ago from the looks of

things, and standing with him, Sarah. They stood side by side but not touching or looking at each other, and Nate could practically feel the tension between them. The photo looked as though it had been taken out in the yard. A black horse with a white blaze stood near Sarah. Fall colors in the deciduous trees indicated it was October or November—after the Labor Day shooting, after Mike got caught up in the life-and-death drama. After things changed. There was nothing written on the back of the picture, but at least it proved Mike had known Sarah and that she was probably exactly who she said she was.

He put the photo down, grabbed the throw from the chair and floated it gently atop Mike. Was Mike dead because he'd been poking around, because he'd been asking questions? How unlikely was that? The kid behind the shooting was dead, so who would care that Mike asked questions?

Jason Netters?

Or was Mike dead because of Sarah? Wasn't it pretty coincidental he should wind up murdered on the very night she came for a visit?

He took the film out of the camera and pocketed it. In the hall closet he found several old jackets, hats and wool scarves, even a fur-lined pair of gloves. He borrowed a little of everything and somehow managed to bend his arm to get it into the jacket. He also found a small flashlight with a good beam.

Behind him, he heard a sharp intake of breath and turned. Sarah stood with her mouth open. "You're wearing his work clothes," she said after a moment. "For a second I thought…" Her voice trailed off as she glanced down at her father's covered form. It crossed Nate's mind to ask her about the photo, but really, what was the point? So far she'd told him very little and the truth of what she had said was open to question. "Where are you going?" she added.

"Outside," he said, moving toward the kitchen. This room was a great deal colder due to the blown-out window.

"Are you sure you're up to that?"

"Yes."

"Well, thank you for covering Dad's body," she added, pausing a few feet away from him.

He turned around and looked at her. "You're welcome. Did your father keep some kind of tool chest in the house?"

"In the laundry room. There's not much in it—or at least there never was."

"Would you get it for me?"

She scooted into the laundry room and returned a second later with a rusty-looking metal box. Opening it revealed a few old nails, a measuring tape, chisel, screwdriver and a hammer. That would have to do.

"What are you up to?" Sarah asked as he chose the tools.

"I'm turning myself into a foreman. Unscrew the biggest cabinet door you can find. That one down there looks about right."

When the board was free, he told her to hold it over the yawning hole where the door windowpane had once been. She hefted it into place and he held it there with one hand while she hammered in every nail they could find. The end result wouldn't win any decorating awards, but at least it gave a sense of security and blocked the cold wind.

"Lock the doors behind me," he cautioned, setting the tools aside.

Her brows furled as she quickly turned, straining to see through the window over the sink, which was acting more like a mirror than a portal. "Why are you going out there? Is the gunman back? Did you hear something?"

"I'm just going to look around. Maybe I'll find something that will tell us who it was and why he left so suddenly. You could save me the effort if you would supply a name and a motive."

She bit her lip as her shoulders rose fractionally. "Sorry."

"I'd dim the lights a little if I were you and stay away from the windows." Without another word, he opened the door, straining against the pile of broken glass that caught under the panel. He switched on the pocket flashlight and shone it into falling snow. Visibility sucked, but recalling where he'd seen the flash of their assailant's shots, he made his way down the cement steps and trudged out into the weather, looking for who knew what.

SARAH STARED AT Nate's retreating figure, then took the small paper-wrapped bundle from where she'd quickly stuffed it out of sight. Unfolding it, she found a silver key. Scribbled on the attached tag was the number 118. Maybe everything she was looking for was in the garage her father rented in Shatterhorn, but she doubted it. He'd sat on his treasure for years—it was extremely unlikely he'd have moved it into a rental unit, of all places.

She rewrapped the key and pushed it back into her pocket, then hurried down the hallway. A few minutes ago, she'd remembered a crawl space above her old closet.

She moved the boxes she'd already emptied out into the room, then shoved the nightstand into the closet to create a makeshift ladder. Climbing up on that, she slid open the panel on the top and then had to take time to track down a flashlight in the kitchen.

The flashlight lit up the crawl space above her room. Not tall enough to be called an attic, just two feet or so into which she'd crammed any number of things when she

was growing up. It was empty now, dusty and dirty, cob-
webs shimmering in the light.

She wasn't sure how long Nate had been gone, just that
time was slipping away at an alarming rate. Once he got
back inside this house, she'd have a horrible time exiting,
and even if she did, what would keep him from tracking
her down?

She climbed off the nightstand and kicked aside the
boxes she'd searched hours before, sick at heart, scared out
of her skull. Then she walked back down the hall.

If the people she feared were behind the shooting, they
would return. She had to leave, storm or no storm, Nate
or no Nate. She took a steadying breath, her mind racing through nonexistent options, searching for a means to
leave and, even as important, a way to salvage her mother's
precarious situation, since Sarah was going to be leaving
without finding what she'd come for.

Unless the key held the answer, but in her gut, she knew
it didn't hold all the answers. It couldn't.

Confide in Nate Matthews.

The thought ran through her mind and it was the only
option that seemed to have even a remote chance of making a difference. He seemed to know how to do everything—no, that was just an illusion created by this insane
situation. He wasn't a superhero; he was just a man—albeit
a very well put-together one with muscles in all the right
places and skin that felt warm even though he had to be as
cold as she was.

That was why she'd trembled. Touching him had been
like opening a window of some kind, like stumbling across
the threshold of an unexpected journey.

All an illusion. Anyway, what could Nate do? What
could anyone do? All he'd want was to detain her because
the bottom line was he was a cop and he thought like one.

On top of that, he was injured. She was first on the scene of a murder. She was obviously evading questions. Why should he trust her? She didn't even trust herself at this point. And hadn't her original plan been to drive him into leaving first?

She had no right to be in her father's house, and yet every right. No right to take what wasn't hers, and yet again, every right. Besides, at this point, what was the difference between right and wrong? What did it matter?

If Nate wasn't here, she could start tearing up the floors and walls. At this point, that was about the only place she hadn't looked except for the acres of land around the house, where anything could be buried. And the ground itself had currently disappeared under the snow.

At the back of her mind, an ugly little question bit at her sanity. Why would someone who wanted the very same thing she was looking for try to shoot her before she found it? The only way that made sense was if he'd already killed her mother and he was cleaning up loose ends. And now she was supposed to try to reason with him? That stood about a zero chance of working, but if not that, what?

All she could do was get out of here and try.

There was one last thing she had to do before she left. Well, two more things. The first one was undoubtedly the most difficult task she'd ever done in her life, but she could not leave her father in the middle of the living room for a whole lot of reasons. The most important one being it was wrong. She'd witnessed Nate taking pictures and studying the scene—that would have to be enough for the police. Lifting his hands, she dragged her father down the hall and into the spare room he used as an office, then got a good-sized blanket from the closet and covered him properly.

For a second, she knelt next to his body. "'Bye, Dad," she whispered. "Maybe this wouldn't have happened if you hadn't double-crossed Mom. Maybe it would have. I don't know. But I'm sorry I wasn't here to save you." She added a silent apology to Nate, too, for what she was about to do to him, then squared her shoulders and did what needed to be done.

Chapter Five

Why had the gunman left?

Nate pondered this question as he tramped through the snow, shining his light every which way, looking for blood or some sign the assailant had been injured and that was why he'd left.

But there was another half inch of accumulated snowfall, and if there had been blood at some point, it was covered now. He found a gaggle of frosty trees, saplings, really, and by the look of them—bent, twisted, broken—he figured this must be where the gunman had turned when he ran away. A few depressions hinted at footsteps and there was a convenient outcropping of boulders nearby for cover.

Nate fell to his knees near the boulder that afforded him the best view of the back of the house. Using his good hand and holding the flashlight between shoulder and chin, he cleared off the new snow. Just when the task was beginning to seem fruitless, his gloved hand passed over something dark that smeared on contact. Blood.

Against all odds, Nate deduced he'd hit the gunman, and despite everything, he sat back on his heels and grinned. About time the good guys scored a point.

Next he followed the trail through the saplings and around some larger trees to a spot with lingering parallel tracks. He recognized the silhouette of the rocks from which he'd leaped and there was a larger depression where he'd fallen. He shone the light over every square inch and caught glimmers of blood. The gunman appeared to have taken a bullet and retreated—at least for the time being. That probably meant he was hurt seriously enough to compromise his ability to fight but not so seriously he couldn't handle a snowmobile.

There was nothing to gain by following the faint tracks, so once again, Nate trudged through the snow, this time shadowing the leftovers of his own earlier trek. He veered off when he made out the looming shape of the barn. It was a relief to get inside out of the weather.

Sarah's rental was the obvious sore thumb in the open area of the structure. He flashed the light around the enclosure until the beam illuminated a switch and he hit it. The lights flickered on, but they were nothing to write home about. Better than burning up batteries, though.

The old green vehicle squatted in front of the closed rolling barn doors. Had Sarah known there was a storm coming? Was that why she'd parked inside the barn? But if she'd only arrived just before he did, then why hadn't he seen tracks on the road when he drove up hours ago? Hers should have still been there, and Mike's murderer's, too, unless he had come the way he'd apparently left, on the snowmobile.

Nate carefully slid into the front seat and looked around. A small suitcase sat on the backseat, while oversize fuzzy pink dice hung from the rearview mirror. A bobblehead blackjack dealer figurine with a green visor leered from the dashboard. Both items seemed incongruous with the personality of the woman he knew as Sarah. They also looked entirely too personal to inhabit a rental car. The keys were lying in a tray between the seats and he took them to keep Sarah from doing something stupid—like trying to drive out of here.

He checked the glove box next, propping his arm on the divider between the seats to take the pressure off his wound. It took him a few minutes to wade through cast-off makeup, brochures, maps, show ticket stubs and casino chips, but he hit pay dirt at the bottom when he came across the car's registration.

"Diana Sarah Donovan," he read aloud, complete with a Reno address. He also found a five-year-old receipt for new tires for this car along with an oil-change schedule that had stopped over two years before, all with Diana Donovan's name somewhere on the forms.

So Sarah went by her middle name. Any way you looked at it, she'd lied about renting the car just like she'd lied about almost everything else.

Nate crammed all the stuff back in the glove box before walking around to the trunk, where he inserted the key. Inside, he found work gloves, rubber boots and a shovel along with an empty cardboard box. Fresh dirt and what appeared to be bits of straw were stuck to the blade of the shovel.

He slammed the lid and rested his right hand on his waist, head tilted, thinking. And as he thought, he began to notice details about the barn he'd missed before. Drawers had been pulled open on the workbench, for instance. Cabinet doors stood ajar. Tool racks had been emptied. Things had been moved away from the walls. He walked down a row of stalls, all empty except the first one, which housed a black horse with a white blaze who looked happy to see him. Skipjack, he presumed.

Nate liked horses. He had four of his own that he rode on the national land that abutted his ranch north of Flagstaff. In fact, there just wasn't anything better than saddling up before dawn and riding out to the river, casting a line and riding home a few hours later with fresh fish for dinner. He'd often wished he'd been a lawman back in the early 1800s, before cars, before automated weapons and incidents like the slaughter of kids at a mall or the most recent tragedy to hit the news, the killing of two sailors on a family beach in Hawaii.

The horse made a friendly grumbling noise in his throat and Nate handed him an apple out of the small barrel outside the stall. He continued on, flashing his light into each successive cubicle. They'd been filled during the years of disuse by an amazing array of broken tools and outdated equipment, but here, too, there were signs an attempt had been made to search each one, at least in a haphazard manner. A shallow hole in one corner explained the shovel, though its purpose was as confusing as everything else.

The horse whinnied, rousing Nate from increasingly troubled thoughts. He left the barn with a sour taste in his mouth, his eyes narrowed, surprised the snow didn't melt in his wake.

A minute later he opened the front door, which he noted Sarah had neglected to lock. It was almost as though she wasn't really afraid, and yet she sure acted nervous. Was it an act or was she just careless?

A third option presented itself when he found her right inside the door, back in her coat, waiting to greet him, the saddle rifle jammed against her right shoulder, the barrel pointed straight at him.

"CLOSE THE DOOR behind you," she said, hating the quiver she detected in her voice.

He did as she'd asked, then looked straight into her eyes. "Do you know how to use that weapon?" he demanded.

"I'll figure it out," she said. "Stop right there."

To her astonishment, he stopped.

"I have to leave," she added for what seemed the twentieth time, glancing at her watch as she spoke, unable to stop herself from obsessing about the minutes ticking away. Behind Nate, she could see the snow still fell, but there was something about it that seemed less intense than it had an hour before. "Close the door and go into the living room," she said.

"Or you'll shoot me?" he asked.

"I'll aim for your foot, but I'm not a marksman, so no promises."

"Not in the chest like your father?"

"I didn't shoot my father."

He looked straight into her eyes. "I know you didn't, Sarah."

"How do you know that?"

He shrugged. "I'm not sure. I guess there's a little corner of my heart that isn't as cynical as you thought. I guess you found your way into it."

She stared into his eyes while tears threatened her own. His comment constituted the one warm moment in this frozen hellhole.

"Or should I call you Diana?" he added.

She blinked. "How—"

"I found the registration in your car."

"It's not mine," she said.

Nate sighed deeply. "You have the upper hand now," he said, closing the door and preceding her into the living room. "Where's your dad's body?" he said, stopping abruptly.

"In the spare room."

"You moved him? Why?"

"Because he deserved something better than getting

stepped around. Because I didn't want to leave you tied up here with Dad lying dead at your feet."

He shook his head, but continued on when she motioned with the gun. "Sit down on that chair," she said, gesturing with the rifle.

He sat down on the straight-backed chair she'd set up by the fireplace and looked up at her. "Like I said, you've got the gun. You're the boss. But why not spend five minutes clearing up a few things before you bolt?" Cradling his injured arm, he nodded at the roll of duct tape she'd found in the laundry room and added, "Then you can tape me to the chair and do whatever you have to do."

Could she really tape this poor guy to a chair, what with his wounded arm and everything else? Hell yes. If that was what she had to do, that was what she had to do. She heard herself say, "Five minutes?"

"That's not too much to ask for a guy who could have gotten himself killed trying to protect you, is it? Besides, what do you have waiting for you? A walk in a snow-storm?"

"That's better than sitting here and wondering what's going on. I hate waiting. I'd rather die trying."

"Well, you may get your chance," he said, imploring her with those sexy eyes. "Five minutes."

As she took a seat opposite him, she noticed the way his broad shoulders drooped, the dark shadows around his eyes. He looked tired, all right, but he didn't look as scared as she figured a man facing a gun should look. She sat down, the rifle at the ready.

"Suppose you could help me take off these gloves?" he asked.

"Sure." She kept the rifle close as she peeled the leather glove from his right hand.

"I can get the other one," he said and pulled gingerly

on the fingers, obviously in pain when the motion jarred his injured arm. She couldn't imagine how he was carrying on as though nothing had happened when it must hurt like hell.

"Okay, now what?" she prompted.

"Let me tell you what I know, and if you want to further enlighten me, that would be great."

"Okay," she said hesitantly.

"I know I wounded our gunman and he left on his snowmobile. I don't know how badly he's hurt, if he went to fix himself up or get reinforcements and is on his way back. I don't know who it is, if the same person killed Mike, or why anyone would want to do any of this."

She nodded.

"I also know you were here last fall. Don't look so startled. There's a relatively recent picture of you and Mike and Skipjack standing out in the yard. It's on top of the mantel."

She glanced over, saw the photo and swore under her breath. How had she managed to overlook that? And yet, how touching that her father had cared enough to stick it up where he could see it once in a while.

"I know you drove here earlier today and parked in the barn, out of sight," Nate continued. "I also know it's your car, that you were looking for something and that from the way you're acting, you haven't found it. How am I doing?"

"Not perfect," she said, but there was a flower of calm beginning to bud in her chest and that in itself should have been setting off alarms. Since getting to Reno two days ago, she'd been moving like a hamster on a wheel and making just about as much progress. Now Nate was close to figuring her out and she almost wanted to help him go the last distance. That was a horrible sign of weakness her mom couldn't afford. Nate's life was law enforcement; he was a man who liked order, who valued the truth. Sarah swallowed hard as her fingers twitched on the gun. "How did you know I got here earlier?"

"There were no tracks on the road when I arrived. The weather must have gone downhill after you pulled into the barn."

She looked away from his intense gaze.

"Your dad didn't even know you were here while you searched the barn, did he?" he added.

She thought before she spoke, weighing the wisdom of engaging in this conversation, deciding at last a little truth couldn't hurt. He'd kind of gotten to her when he'd expressed that unwarranted—from his point of view—faith in her. She'd remain wary and on the defensive, but a little chat couldn't hurt, could it? "He wasn't home when I got here."

"Obviously, he returned."

"Obviously. I heard his truck. I knew he was planning on driving into Shatterhorn this afternoon, so I was surprised he'd come back to the ranch."

"You knew his plans?"

"Yeah. I talked to him a couple of days ago."

"So you chose a time to visit when he'd be gone."

One of her shoulders lifted a little. Man, she sounded like a coldhearted bitch, even to her own ears. Of course, her dad hadn't helped any.

"Because you needed to find something that you didn't want him to know you were looking for," Nate added.

"More or less. My plan was to search the house first, but he came home almost at once, so I started with the barn. After a while, I heard another car and looked outside again. A silver sedan had parked next to Dad's old truck. A man was just going into the house."

Nate suddenly straightened in the chair, his gaze sharpening. "Who was it?" he asked.

"I don't know."

"But it might have been his killer."

"I know that now. If I'd run outside maybe I could have stopped Dad's murder, but at the time, I just thought it was a friend or something."

"What kind of car was it?"

She shrugged. "A newish one. I don't know what model or make. I only saw it from the side, so I'm not sure if it had a Nevada plate. And before you ask, I never saw the man's face. I didn't really see anything except his legs disappearing into the house."

"What was he wearing?"

"I don't know. Wait. Black boots. A long coat."

"What did you do then?"

"Put my stuff back in the trunk in case Dad came out here and found me and then just hung out with Skipjack, waiting for the other guy to leave. I wasn't really anxious to see Dad, so I kind of hoped he'd just go away with the guy if I gave him time. For all I knew, his plans had changed and Dad had invited the man to the ranch."

"And then?"

She started to speak, then paused, her eyes moist again. It was hard to get the words out.

"Take your time," Nate said softly, his voice tender in a way that further undid her. Tears threatened to roll down her cheeks and she sucked them back.

"I fell asleep," she said.

"What?"

She took a deep breath. "I just fell asleep. It had been a horrible forty-eight hours leading up to that point. I'd closed the door to the stall and it was relatively warm and there was fresh straw…. Dad must have done that earlier. The horse kind of snuffled around and I closed my eyes. The next thing I knew, Skipjack was blowing hot air on my face and it was darker inside the barn. I got up and peeked outside. The weather had really deteriorated since I'd last looked. A couple of hours or more must have passed.... The silver car was gone and Dad's truck was still where he'd parked it. I didn't know if Dad had left with the other guy or not, but I knew I needed to check."

"Why did you need to check all of a sudden?" Nate asked. "You'd been content to stay hidden up to that point."

"I had a dream," she said, amazed with herself for sharing this. "In my dream someone…well, someone I feel responsible for was drowning and I couldn't help. I was frozen in place. Powerless. When I woke up, I admitted to myself that I needed Dad's help, and if he was still here, I had to go ask for it." She didn't tack on the word *again,* but it played in her mind.

"Why would he have refused to help you?" Nate asked gently.

She equivocated just a little. "You have to understand that we parted on a really sour note last fall. We both said things— Well, it's too late for regrets, but I still have them. Lately, we'd been talking by phone and he just started to get odder and odder."

"Like how?"

She took a deep breath. "He talked about Pearl Harbor a lot. He was way too young to have ever been in World War II and I know he's never been to Hawaii, so I didn't get what he was going on about. Maybe he wanted to move. I don't know. Then he started going on about Washington. I explained I had moved from there to Virginia, but he passed that off as though I hadn't even spoken. He was impatient and scattered—I mean, he was all over the map. Talking about the newspaper articles written after the shooting and the mayor of Shatterhorn and how you and he and that other guy had been called patriots for what you did. I really began to think the shootings had unhinged him."

"I know what you mean," Nate said softly. "His emails were getting bizarre."

"Exactly. He was obsessed with reading about terrorist groups and civilian militia movements and a whole bunch of other stuff. Like I said, I know he'd been hounding everybody. Then he went off on a group called People's Liberation. He was sure they were behind some incident—"

"The shooting in Hawaii last December," Nate interjected. "Maybe that's why he was talking about Pearl Harbor. The victims were off-duty sailors."

"Then you know about this group's involvement?"

"I've read things. Some believe their claims, some don't. The Hawaiian shooter was an out-of-work malcontent who had been rejected by the navy. No one ever heard about any motive he might have had. But what did Mike think the newspaper editor of a small Nevada town could do about any of this?"

"I don't know, Nate. I have to admit I tuned him out after a while."

Nate nodded. The look in his eyes made her think that he, too, had occasionally tuned out her father's ranting.

"Okay, so you were going to go talk to him. Then what?"

"I walked across the yard and found Dad's front door open. That seemed really ominous because it was cold and snowing." She paused again, catching her breath. "Dad was right where you found him. I'd never seen any dead person before, let alone someone I…I was close to, so I felt for a pulse, but I think I knew he was already gone. I also knew there was nothing I could do for him and that time was running out for me to save my— So, I…I started searching the house, you know, to see if he'd been robbed."

Nate cocked an eyebrow. "That's why you searched the house?"

She looked away and didn't respond directly. "I found his computer was gone along with a notebook he used to jot things down. I looked to see if there was anything else missing, thought of the safe, and that's where I was when I heard you arrive. You know the rest."

Nate shook his head. "No, as a matter of fact, I don't know the rest. What are you looking for and why? Who are you trying to protect? Why are you lying about owning the car? What difference does it make?"

Sarah leaned toward him, fighting the desire to lay her troubles before this near stranger.

"You have to know how this is going to look to the cops when they're finally notified," he continued. "Your unwillingness to be up front concerning your father's murder makes it look like you were in cahoots with someone and that someone killed your father and now you're protecting him or her. Can't you see that?"

She stood up, the gun at the ready. The back of her nose ached with building pressure; her hands trembled. Of course she knew all this, and when he said how it would look to the cops, he meant how it looked to him because he was a cop. He didn't believe her at all; he was just trying to get her to talk.

"I can't tell you anything else," she said. "It's not my information to share. I'm leaving now. Don't try to stop me. I don't want to hurt you."

Like a striking rattlesnake, he reached up and shoved the barrel of the gun downward with his right hand before twisting it out of her grip.

He was suddenly standing in front of her, his face strained and shadowed. He set the rifle aside and clutched her upper arm with his good hand. "There's a greater enemy than me running around, but you know that, don't you?"

"I could have killed you!" she cried, her whole body shaking now. "What kind of madman grabs a rifle that way?"

"The kind who knows there's no round in the chamber and bets there's no more ammunition in the house," he said. "The kind who is tired of whatever game you're playing."

"It's not a game," she said.

"Don't tell me. Tell your dead father," Nate responded.

She raised her hand to slap him and he caught it. Before she could protest, he'd taken care of quieting her by pulling her closer and covering her lips with his. She attempted to wrench free, but his grip tightened, and then it relaxed and she knew she could tear herself away now, that he'd had a chance to think about his actions and probably regret them.

But she didn't budge.

Chapter Six

For a moment, Nate lost track of time and place. Sarah had fought to get away for about two seconds, and then she'd melted against him. By the time they'd moved into a second kiss, he was as good as lost in a blizzard. There was nothing but the silky moistness of Sarah's mouth, the feel of her breasts pressed against his chest. Gradually, her arm encircled his neck and her fingers grazed his cheek. A dizzying flood of sensations bombarded his nervous system. He forgot about Mike's murder, about gunmen and craziness and crashes in the night and being shot and bloodied. He even forgot about evasions and secrets and lies and uncertainty, all for one glorious minute.

The next time she pulled away, he let her. She didn't go far, and when he looked down at her, there was a speculative gleam in her eyes that wrapped itself around his heart. He'd been fighting awareness of her since the moment he'd met her and she'd made it easier by being so blasted contrary, but here it was, rushing through his blood, pounding in his veins. He kissed her again, softly, the need for her surging through his body.

Nate wasn't sure if Sarah allowed him this intimacy because she figured that was the best way to control him or if she'd been as jolted as he by the events of the past few hours. All he was sure of was that he'd kissed his fair

share of women in his life, been married to one and engaged to another, and it had never, ever happened like this.

"Do they teach you to kiss like that in police school?"
she whispered, running her fingers lightly across his lips.

"Basic interrogation 101," he said.

"I bet you aced the class."

He smiled to himself, and not just because the conversation was silly and he knew he was acting like a moron, but
because the sound of her voice did that to him. He didn't
know a whole lot about her but he did know that on some
level, he *knew* her.

"I'm sorry I pointed a gun at you," she said with a quick
upsweep of her lashes. "Is it really empty?"

"Yep. That's why I didn't take it with me when I went
outside to scout."

"I thought you'd forgotten it."

"Cops don't forget their weapons," he said, ignoring
the irony of the comment. He hadn't forgotten his gun;
he'd chosen to leave it behind in some crazy mind game
he was playing with himself. He let that thought go when
he sensed her leaning in toward him again. He lowered his
head a little and she raised hers. Electricity arced between
them as his lips throbbed with anticipation.

They both heard the noise at the same time, a loud crashing and a crack coming from outside as the lights blinked
out and the house plunged into silent darkness. Sarah's
gasp sent shivers down Nate's spine. A second later, her
footsteps pounded across the wood floor, away from him.

He groped his way toward her, at a loss to remember
exactly where the furniture was. He sped up when he heard
the door open and a shade of lighter gray appeared. Was
she choosing this moment to try to run away again? If she
was, he was about ready to let her go.

"Show yourself!" he heard her shout.

He switched on the flashlight he'd pocketed when coming inside and found Sarah standing out in the middle of the yard, yelling into the night. If someone was out here, she made a perfect target, as a subtle break in the weather allowed weak gray moonlight to filter down through the trees.

"Do you hear me!" she screamed again. "Are you out here? Answer me!"

Something overhead made a creaking, groaning noise that captured Nate's attention. He shone the light overhead, where he caught a glimpse of a sagging power line. He followed it along until the raw wood of a fresh break high in an evergreen laden with fresh snow stood out like a sore thumb. The break had sent a limb the size of a shopping-mall Christmas tree crashing down on the lines below, yanking on a utility pole, which now leaned at a crazy angle.

Beside him, Sarah yelled again, all but shaking her fist, twirling around every which way. He caught her shoulder and turned her to face him. Tears sparkled on her cheeks. Her eyes looked huge and manic.

"I can't take it anymore," she said, flicking the tears away, looking over his shoulder as though the marauders were close at hand. "Whoever he is, let him come out in the open and announce what he wants!"

"Who?" Nate asked. "Give me a name."

"I can't give you a name. I don't know it. But he's out here. I can feel it in my bones."

"I don't think so," Nate said. "Look." He shone the light and she followed its beam up to the treetops. "It's the power line," he added. "The sound we heard was the wood breaking. The branch got too heavy, but this may be good news. The utility company may send out a crew to fix it."

"How can they help us?" she asked, her voice full of despair.

"I'm not sure," he told her. "On the other hand, anyone not shooting us is better than no one. Come on, let's go back inside. We need to find a better light source than flashlights."

"There are lanterns in the barn," she said.

"Great."

The barn was darker than the outside. The horse must have been spooked by the crashing noise not far from his stall or the sound of Sarah shouting or both, because they could hear him snorting and kicking his stall walls.

"The lanterns are in that cabinet over there," Sarah said. "I'm going to go check on Skipjack."

Nate assumed she either knew where the lanterns were because they'd been there during her childhood or because she'd run across them when she'd searched the place hours before. He found two that seemed to have all their parts and fuel, as well. He lit one of them and it emitted a warm, yellow glow.

"I opened the door to the outside pasture," Sarah said when she finally returned.

She looked hauntingly beautiful in the light from the lantern and it was all he could do not to pull her into his arms. What in the world was happening to him and why did it have to happen now and with this woman?

"Why did you do that?" He handed her a lantern.

"Just in case. I don't want him stuck in here if, well…"

"I'd like to reassure you that we're going to be fine, but without knowing what's really going on, that seems like a naive statement. And you don't strike me as a naive woman, Sarah Donovan."

"No, I'm not," she said, her gaze flitting away under his scrutiny.

"How are you connected to the people you think are behind this?" When she didn't respond, he added, "You know, maybe you could try accepting a little help."

"The price is too high," she said.

"There is no price."

"There's always a price. Besides, you're a lawman."

He bit back a disclaimer. "I'm also a man stuck inside an incredibly volatile situation," he reminded her. "And believe it or not, I do know how to think outside the box." He lit the other lantern and lifted it with his good arm. The jarring motion of stripping the gun away from her followed by everything else had set his shoulder aching anew.

"Let me think," she said softly, turning away from him.

"Just think fast," he warned her. "Sooner or later, someone will return to finish what he started."

"I know."

As they made their way toward the barn door, the light illuminated the green sedan. This time, Nate noticed the faded sticker on the rear bumper: Life Is a Casino, it said. He shook his head. "It's kind of hard to associate what I know of you with fuzzy pink dice and gambling slogans."

He was aware of the deep breath she drew. "It's not my car."

"Right. I keep forgetting that," he said, increasingly frustrated with her.

"It belongs to my mother," she added. "Her first name is Diana. Sarah was her mother's name. It's who I'm named after."

"Why couldn't you just tell me you had your mother's car?" Nate asked. "What's the big secret about that, or did you take it without asking?"

"Trust me, she knows I have it. I lied about it because you're a cop and Mom is mixed up in some pretty dicey stuff."

"And you're trying to help her?"

Sarah nodded.

"That's why you came here. To look for something for her?"

"Yes," she said and, quickening her pace, preceded him out of the barn.

"Were you followed?" he called, but she didn't respond.

He caught up with her halfway across the yard, though she was moving fast.

"Were you followed?" he asked again.

"I don't think so," she said. "I was really careful."

"Then how could whoever this is wind up here, of all places?"

The answer was slow in coming, as though she had to reach deep inside to drag it up her throat and push it out of her mouth. "Maybe Mom told him this is where I was headed."

Nate took her arm and propelled her into the house. There was no better target on a dark night than someone standing still while holding a light. Two such someones just upped the odds.

He closed and locked the door. "Sarah, you need help," he said as he set his lantern down on top of the counter-high divider between entry and living room. "You know that, right? You were willing to risk asking your father. Can't you extend that trust? Let me help you."

"You promise you won't arrest me?"

"I can't arrest anyone in Nevada," he said. *Or anywhere else.*

"You can make trouble for me and I can't afford the luxury of time to straighten things out. I have to find what I came for and return it to Reno or get back there and try to reason with someone who strikes me as really unreasonable."

"Reason with the person who's been taking potshots at us? Do you really think you can?"

"I don't have any other choice. I can't find the coins."

There it was—the object of her search was coins. "Valuable coins?"

She turned her head, her jaw set in a stubborn line.

"For heaven's sake, Sarah, just spit it out."

Her next look was defiant. "Okay. Yes, coins."

"Old coins? Doubloons? Come on, give me a break," he pleaded.

"Silver coins my great-grandfather collected."

"A lot of them?"

"Scads."

He stared at her and finally took a deep breath. "I'm waiting. Define *scads*."

"Rolls of them," she said. "All stacked into three-gallon coffee cans. Dad told me stories about how Grandpa stood in line to buy them when they were first minted. My grandfather passed them along to my father, who refused to put them in a bank because he wanted to keep them close by. He wouldn't even spend them, just liked knowing he had them. 'Rainy-day coins,' he called them, even after the ranch started going downhill and he had to sell the horses. His truck is broken-down, the house is falling apart… Exactly what kind of rainy day was he waiting for?"

"I don't know," Nate said uselessly.

"At any rate, each silver dollar is worth at least two or three hundred dollars. I've looked everywhere, but I can't find them."

"And you need this silver to do what?"

She set her lantern on the fireplace hearth, then plopped down on an ottoman, landing in a heap. She raised both hands in a hopeless gesture and mumbled, "Save my mother. She's in big trouble with some very bad people."

"What kind of trouble?"

"She's addicted to gambling, Nate," Sarah said with a darted look to his face as if admitting a flaw in her own personality. "This time she got into a real mess when she burned up her credit lines with even the semireputable lenders. She had to go to this loan-shark guy."

"I take it that's the guy you think is shooting at us?"

"No, the loan shark is a man named Jack Poulter. He would never dirty his own hands."

"Now I'm confused," Nate said.

"Poulter demanded payment. When Mom admitted she didn't have enough to repay him, he warned her that no one walked away from debts owed him. She said something like, 'You can't get blood out of a turnip.' I gather he disagreed with her. Still, she thought she'd charm her way out of it."

"Really? Loan sharks aren't exactly famous for allowing someone to screw around with them."

"You don't know my mother. I think she just thought he'd view the whole thing as a big mistake and let it go."

"But he didn't."

"Of course not. He disappeared from the front line, so to say, but within a day or so, a stranger showed up at my mom's house. He said he was there to enforce Poulter's claim for a percentage and he had no intention of walking away empty-handed."

"Who was it?"

"He gave the name Bellows. That's all. He's a scary-looking guy with a couple of silver teeth. He had another guy with him."

"I don't understand. Why would Poulter loan your mother that much money in the first place? Did she have collateral?"

"Dad gave her one of the coffee cans when they split, on the condition she would completely relinquish any interest in this ranch. She burned up most of that money, but some was tied up in a CD. As I understand it, this time she took a loan on what she optimistically considered a 'sure thing' using the CD money as collateral, telling Poulter she had a whole lot more than she really did. When the money was gone and the sure thing fizzled out, she was left holding the bag. After Bellows showed up, Mom got creative and asked Dad to bail her out. I guess he agreed and then changed his mind. He told her this time she'd have to face the consequences of her actions."

"'This time'?"

"This has been an ongoing pattern for her as long as I can remember. She's spent her life moving between self-made disasters. I tried to distance myself from her by moving east, but she always seems to find a way to reel me back in. I haven't actually seen her in months."

Nate considered his next question carefully. "You're sure your dad still has these coins?"

"Pretty sure. He agreed to give Mom the money when she asked him, and he knew it was up to almost a quarter of a million dollars, so he must have had it."

Nate whistled. "That's a lot of money."

"Tell me about it."

"Your mother couldn't mortgage her house or—"

Sarah interrupted him with a laugh devoid of mirth. "What house? She lost that years ago. Her net worth is less than zero, way less, and she tapped me dry the last time she got in bad trouble. It wasn't a lot, but it was all I had. I'd been working for years, saving money to go back to college. It took every penny to get her solvent."

Did Sarah understand how she was enabling her mother? "That many coins are going to be very heavy," he said. "You won't be able to walk them out of here."

"I know."

"What really happened to your ID?"

Sarah rubbed her eyes. "Bellows snatched my purse. He didn't want me going too far. That's why I couldn't rent a car and had to take Mom's."

"How long before this guy acts on his threats?"

"Tomorrow at three o'clock. Then he says he'll cut his losses."

"And you believe that means he'll harm her?"

"He broke two of her fingers to convince her to call me for help. I don't know if he'll kill her outright, but I'd bet the ranch he'll take out his frustration in a brutal way, and I don't know how much more she can stand."

"But why call you? They didn't think you had that kind of money, did they?"

"Mom must have told him she had to travel to get the money and he didn't trust her. So he roughed her up until she agreed to ask someone else to go on her behalf. That turned out to be me. This dude met me at the airport, showed me a picture of my mother all beaten and bloody, demanded my purse and gave me the keys to her car along with directions to be back tomorrow by three o'clock. For all intents and purposes, I'm now her hostage. If she bolts and goes to the cops, they come after me."

Nate shook his head. As devious as Sarah had proved herself to be, he believed her. The past few hours had taken a lot out of both of them and he doubted she was up to inventing all of this. "If these people are expecting you to produce that much money, why would they try to kill you? Why not just wait until you brought it back?"

"I don't know. The only thing I can figure is that he made

Mom tell him where I was going to get the money. She must have said I was going to get it from her ex-husband. If he got wind that there was a lot more here than what Mom technically owes, he'll want every penny of it." She sat forward and added, "I have to either find the silver or figure out a way to extend the deadline. Otherwise, my mother is dead, I'm dead and now it looks like you're dead, too. It's as simple as that."

Chapter Seven

Nate's brow furrowed as he looked into Sarah's eyes.

It didn't make sense to him that men as ruthless as these guys had orchestrated the present situation. There was the fact that someone had come into Mike's house and killed him in cold blood but never even looked in the barn to see if anyone else was here. Then, after killing Mike, why did he drive away and come back on a snowmobile? He would probably have had to rent it and that would be traceable when all was said and done. It just seemed sloppy.

But thugs weren't always the most organized of people, and if the gunman was Bellows's lackey, he might be making this up as he went along.

Sarah rubbed her eyes, suppressing a yawn in the process. Running a hand through her hair, she stood and took off her jacket, then offered to help him with his. Although he dreaded moving the arm again, he agreed. The coat came off with a few internalized gasps on Nate's part and a glistening layer of sweat on his brow. Sarah studied his sleeve for a moment in the flickering lantern light and then met his gaze. "Your arm is bleeding again."

"I figured."

"Come on, I'll fix you up."

She grabbed one of the lanterns and he followed her down the dimly lit hall back to the bedroom. He sat down on the bed and began fumbling with his shirt buttons while she went into the bathroom to wash her hands. "Let me help you do that," she said, deftly interceding once she returned. The process was much as before, except that this time they'd recently shared a few kisses and everything seemed charged with awareness. When she peeled the shirt away from his arm, she frowned. He glanced down and saw the bandage had turned red.

"You need to go to bed for a few days," she said.

"That's not going to happen," he said as she unwound the bandage and dropped it in the trash can. She smeared antibiotic cream on a pad, which she placed directly over the wound, then she rebandaged his arm. A couple of seconds later, she'd produced another clean shirt from her father's drawers and helped Nate slide his arm into the sleeve. Mike had been shorter and heavier than Nate, so the sleeves ended above his wrist bones.

"I'll make you a sling out of a bedsheet," she said as she buttoned his shirt. Technically, he could have done two-thirds of these things himself, but the truth was he enjoyed her fussing over him. She disappeared into the hall and re-entered carrying a white sheet, which she tore into pieces to fashion a sling. When she tied it around his neck, he reached up to touch her face and she glanced down at him.

"Thanks," he said.

Her smile was warm and quick. She sat down beside him and put her head against his good shoulder. "I'm the one who should be thanking you," she murmured. She looked up into his eyes and added, "Don't you wish we could just lie down on this bed and go to sleep for a few hours?"

"Yes to the lying down," he said, kissing her softly on the lips. "No to the sleeping."

"And with that arm, how would you go about making love to me? That is what you're talking about, isn't it?"

"Yes it is," he said. "And the answer is I would go about it very carefully but with abandon."

"I thought you were engaged to be married."

"I was. Now I'm not."

"What happened?"

"A few weeks ago I told her I was coming up here to see my friends and she just fell apart. She said I wasn't the same as I'd been, that I was living in the past, that I'd come home from Shatterhorn a different man."

"You, too? Like Dad?"

"Not exactly, but changed. I lost a little of my swagger, wasn't so sure I was leading the life I wanted or that I had all the answers. I failed to save two kids, Sarah. I was there after a vacation, unarmed and vulnerable, and I let two kids die. If I'd been carrying, the whole thing would have ended a lot differently."

"But that wasn't your fault…."

"Maybe not technically, but saving innocent people is what I'm supposed to be able to do, and I failed. I guess I was so disappointed in myself that it affected other parts of my life and I kind of closed down."

"But it's only been a few months, Nate. You have to give yourself a chance. Anyone who goes through a mess like that is going to suffer some changes, don't you think? Your girl should have stood by you and helped you."

He shrugged. "She's a little on the impatient side. She wanted me to be who I was before, and I couldn't do it. Enough about me. What happened to the cop you married?"

"We got hitched when I was seventeen. That's right after Mom's gambling worsened. Dad told her to leave. I had just graduated from high school and I didn't know what to do."

"So you got married?"

"It was more complicated than that," she said softly.

"In what way?"

"We saw each other through some hard times," she said.

"You didn't take his name?"

"No. I had all these dreams of being a veterinarian and I wanted my own name—at least that's what I told myself—but I think I really kept it in an attempt to make my dad proud of me. I always disappointed him."

"That seems so unlikely," Nate said.

She smiled. "Well, that's how it seemed to me at the ripe old age of seventeen. You didn't really know Dad well, did you?"

"No, not at all."

"He could be hard. I mean, as strange as he got, the truth is he was always a little on the odd side and his temper—Well, he had a temper."

"Was your husband like your dad?"

"No, no way. Johnny was kind. He had a good heart."

"What happened between you guys?"

"He left me," Sarah said. "Not by choice, though. He was shot in the line of duty and died before I could get to him."

"I'm so sorry," Nate said softly. He stared at her for several seconds. The light bathed her face with a glow that made her seem otherworldly, too beautiful to be human, too human to be anything else. There was sadness in her tilted blue eyes that he yearned to kiss away. She was so alive her body seemed to hum.

And she was in deep trouble....

"Where did your father used to keep the coins?" he asked.

"The only time I ever saw them, they were in a secret cabinet built into the wall beside the fireplace."

"I assume that's the first place you looked?"

"Absolutely. There's nothing in there now but a photo of Skipjack."

"From the looks of things, you've searched just about everywhere else."

"I tried, but you arrived before I could tackle the floors and walls."

"That's why you were looking in the safe?"

She paused a second.

"I know you took something out of the safe," he told her. "I saw you put it in your pocket."

"Oh, that," she said. "It's nothing. Nothing to do with the coins or my mother, anyway. It's just a key and it's personal."

He nodded. "Okay. Nothing else in the safe, though, right?"

"No. I was hoping the coins themselves would be in there or maybe a clue as to where he might have moved them. Even proof he sold them would be better than nothing. And I wanted to find his will, too, but it wasn't in there, either."

"I guess we better continue the search, then."

"We?" she asked.

"I'm not going anywhere," he said. "In fact, if you want to lie down and close your eyes for a few minutes, I'll take all the pictures off the walls and look for any sign things were disturbed, like new plaster or patches. It'll be daylight in a few hours, and one way or another, we have to get out of here or reinforce our position, so we need to work fast."

"Then I'll help," she said and got to her feet. She offered him a hand and pulled him up beside her. They stared at each other a moment, Nate a little dizzy. She caught his good shoulder with her hand. "You okay?"

"Dandy," he said and, leaning forward, gently kissed her forehead.

For the next thirty minutes, they stripped everything off the walls. Studying every surface with flashlights, they found absolutely nothing alarming or suggestive except faded spots on the paint, which clearly indicated each wall hanging had been in place for umpteen years.

"Any of the rugs new?" Nate asked as he sank down on the edge of the sofa. Sarah had done all the heavy work, but he was still hurting.

"You mean since I was a kid? A few. The area rug in the living room, the one in my old bedroom and the wall to wall in the master bedroom."

"Let's get to it," Nate said. "We're going to need a crowbar."

"There's one in the barn."

"I saw it on the workbench. I'll go get it."

She shook her head as she looked at him. "Not this time. You rest your arm. I'll go get it."

"And will you come back?" he asked, challenging her gaze.

She smiled. "Maybe, maybe not." A second later, she was gone.

Sarah, hurrying as fast as the weather and growing fatigue allowed, paused as she entered the barn.

Her mother's old green sedan squatted there like a bloated toad. A couple of hours before, she would have tried to drive it out of here and probably gotten stuck in the snow. It wasn't that she was an idiot; it was inaction that was slowly killing her. That and wondering what was happening back in Reno. And truth be known, even now she was tempted to hop in the car and give it a try.

But she couldn't leave Nate here. Her gut told her this

wasn't over. They had to find the coins and get them out of here before someone returned.

She found the crowbar and hurried back across the yard. The snow was coming in flurries now, cold but dry. In the pasture to her left, she heard Skipjack's heavy breathing as he galloped across the pasture toward her, probably hoping for a handout.

She reentered the house, locking the door behind her. Nate looked up from where he knelt beside the fireplace cabinet.

"You came back," he said, and it was impossible not to note the pleasure in his voice.

"Yeah, well, it amazes me, too." She crossed the room and squatted beside him. "What are you doing?"

"I was just looking at this cabinet. It all but disappears when it's closed. I didn't know Mike was such a crafts-man."

"He wasn't. My grandfather built this house."

Nate got to his feet and offered Sarah a hand. "Let's start pushing aside rugs and pulling up floors."

Because of his injury, Sarah did most of the physical labor. It actually felt good to put energy into something besides worrying, and she tackled the wood floor in the living room with abandon. They were old tongue-and-groove fir boards, soft but thick, and pretty soon it became very clear it would take days to tear up all the floor.

Eventually, they changed their tactics and began moving aside rugs and looking for any changes in the flooring, like a patch or different wood. They ended up back in the living room where they'd started.

"I wish he'd left those cans in that cabinet," Sarah said bitterly.

"I wonder why he moved them."

"Probably because Mom knew where they were and he

didn't trust her not to rob him. Isn't that a laugh? Here I am, robbing him on her behalf."

"Unless there's someone I don't know about, I would assume they'd be yours now anyway."

"Maybe. Or maybe he intended to give them to a good cause or his friends. Who knows?"

"When your mother took your college money, why didn't Mike help you? I mean, if he had all this money, I'd think he'd want to support your dreams."

"I couldn't tell him what Mom did."

"Why?"

"Because I had to protect her."

He stared down at her. "Isn't that supposed to work both ways? Isn't she supposed to look out for you, too?"

Sarah shrugged and looked away. "It doesn't exactly work that way in my family."

Nate let it drop as he knelt again, and this time when he stood, he held the snapshot of Skipjack in his hand. "Why was this one lone photograph in that cabinet?" he asked.

"I don't know."

"Is it an important picture?"

Sarah took the photograph and studied it. "Well, as you can see, it's Skipjack. See that upside-down horse-shoe above his stall door? Dad said the string holding it up there rotted away about two years ago and it never got remounted, so the picture is at least that old. So, no, I can't say if there's anything special about the photo."

"Sarah," Nate said, his voice soft and slow. "What if your dad hid the coins in the horse's stall?"

She looked up at him, her grip on the crowbar tight. "That could be it," she said, hope ringing in her head. She lifted one of the lanterns in her free hand. "Come on."

Once again, they put their coats on and trudged across the yard and into the barn, hurrying now, Sarah afraid to think it through because she couldn't bear to face potential holes in this last-ditch theory. She closed the bottom half of the outside door to the horse's stall to keep him from coming back inside and getting in their way. Nate found a pitchfork.

"Let me do that," she said, taking the tool from him. "This is two-handed work."

"Okay, you clear the floor, and I'll check the walls. Okay if I take down that hay rack?"

"Sure."

They each set to work as the black-and-white horse hung his head over the open panel and watched. Within a few minutes Nate had used the crowbar one-handed to take the hay rack off the wall and Sarah had shifted all the straw out of the stall.

"Nothing," Nate said, his voice weary.

Sarah didn't trust herself to speak. The dirt floor looked the same as in the rest of the barn. Nate shined his flashlight along the walls, and it glittered on something metallic, which caught their attention. Moving closer, Sarah identified the old horseshoe. It was hanging on the wall above where the hay rack had once been and the ground beneath it looked freshly disturbed.

"I'm getting the shovel out of my trunk," she said.

"Wait a second," Nate said, digging in his pocket. "You'll need your keys."

She shook her head as she took them from him. He'd known she wasn't leaving or even going to try to when she looked for the crowbar, because he'd had the keys all along.

She returned with work gloves and tools. "I have a feeling about the floor right here," Sarah said, and hefting the shovel, she slammed it down into the dirt. It penetrated the earth. She immediately put some muscle behind the spade and began digging.

She was about ready to admit defeat when the blade hit something that made a thumping, hollow sound. Working faster now, she quickly shoveled the dirt away to reveal a painted wooden trapdoor, which she hastily cleared of dirt before falling to her knees. Nate brought the lantern closer.

There was a handle set into the wood with a small chain attached to it. Nate leaned down and grabbed the chain, raising the lid. The link on the end of the chain was just long enough to slip over one end of the horseshoe to keep it open.

Sarah peered into a hole that appeared to be about two feet deep and three feet across, hollowed out of the earth and reinforced with bricks. Best of all, the shine of metal cans dazzled in her eyes.

"There have to be ten or eleven of them down here," she said, her voice hushed, her heart racing. She swallowed a sob of relief.

"Do you need help lifting them out?" Nate asked, peering over her shoulder.

"No, I can do it."

Years before, her father had poked opposing holes near the tops of the cans through which he'd threaded nylon rope, thus creating handles so they could be easily lifted. Sarah stretched out on her stomach and hooked one with her hand. Her heart sank as she realized it wasn't nearly heavy enough to hold coins.

Nate sat down on the stall floor beside her.

"Is that one of them?"

"No, it's too light. But it's the same kind of can I remember." She sat up, took off the leather gloves and opened the plastic lid. Nate shined a flashlight into the can and Sarah withdrew a few folded sheets of paper stapled together in one corner. Next came a small brown notebook wrapped in purple rubber bands. She handed Nate the notebook and unfolded the papers.

"This is his will," she said as she held the sheets toward the light to read. After a few moments of silence, she added, "He left me everything."

"Then even if the coins are gone, you'll have the ranch and the land," Nate said.

"Yeah. Maybe I can bargain for Mom's life with it. This could help me buy her a little more time." She refolded the papers and slipped them into her jacket pocket, then nodded at the book in Nate's hands. "That's his notebook, isn't it?"

He tried to hand it to her but she stopped him. "That's okay. You look at it. You were with him at the mall shooting. Maybe his ramblings will mean something to you."

"I'll study it later," he said, shining the light at the rest of the cans. "Well, let's get it over with," he added as he lowered his good arm into the hole and hooked another rope. He glanced back over his shoulder at Sarah. "This one is really heavy. I bet it weighs forty pounds."

"I hope it's not full of rocks," Sarah said, holding her breath again as he yarded an old red coffee can from the hole.

Sarah's mouth was dry as Nate pried open the lid. And there they were, roll upon roll of coins that looked as though they'd never even been unwrapped.

"Wow," Nate said on an expelled breath. "There have to be thirty rolls in here." He pulled one out carefully and handed it to Sarah.

The coins were wrapped in heavy brown paper, the ends partially open to reveal the brilliant gleam of silver. The paper was stamped *Carson City Mint*.

"Twenty coins a roll," Nate said. "Uncirculated, to boot. That means each can is worth at least one hundred and fifty thousand dollars and there are—" he paused to count "—ten more of them. If they all hold the same amount, you're talking over one and a half million dollars."

Sarah felt a giggle tickle her throat as despair turned into hope. "Now all we have to do is figure out how to get them away from here."

"That's all," Nate said.

They were silent for a moment, and in that moment, Skipjack whinnied and trotted away from the barn, the sound of his hooves moving fast and sure and toward the part of the pasture that fronted the house. They were both still sitting on the floor, the lantern on the ground with them and the top panel of Skipjack's stall opened to the wooded area behind the barn. There was an ominous quiet as they both got to their feet and looked outside the stall door, but the house wasn't visible from this angle and everything looked peaceful enough.

"I hear something," Sarah said.

"Shh," Nate warned her, dousing the lantern light. He left the stall in a hurry, moving toward the front of the barn. Sarah knew he was trying to get a better view. Sheltering the beam of her flashlight with her hand, she quickly picked up her father's notebook and stuffed it inside her jacket, tucked the roll of coins she still held back in the can and deposited both cans in the hole. Working as quietly as she could, she closed the trapdoor and quickly covered it with dirt, then, using the pitchfork, put down a heavy layer of straw. She couldn't risk the noise of reattaching the hay rack, so she propped it up instead and stuck hay in it. Then she opened the bottom half of the outside stall door before turning and running to the front of the barn, where she found Nate's dark form peering through the slats in the door.

"What is it?" she whispered, coming up to stand beside him.

"I think someone is behind the house. I saw lights and heard an engine. I'm going to go investigate."

"Nate, no, please don't. You're unarmed and you're hurt. Let's just wait here. We can defend the barn if we have to—"

She got no further, because in that instant, they both saw flames licking the side of the house.

Chapter Eight

Sarah cried out. "Dad!"

Nate slid a hand over her mouth and drew her against him, talking softly and close to her ear. "The fire can't hurt him, Sarah. We have to get out of here."

"The snow is still too deep for the car."

"We'll take the horse. Can you saddle him?"

"Yes." She tore herself from his grasp and ran into the dark. Nate took one last look at the burning house. Through the now lightly falling snow, he caught the shape of a man standing off to the side, visible because of the light created from the fire. He stood at a point where it was likely he could see both the front and the back doors, and he had what appeared to be a rifle clutched in his hands. Nate could make out the front half of a snowmobile parked behind him.

It was obvious to Nate that the guy was waiting to pick off whoever ran from the house when they realized it was on fire. When no one showed up, would it finally dawn on him to check the barn?

Turning, Nate moved as fast as he dared. He didn't know his way around the barn as well as Sarah did and there was no way he would risk a light until he was buried in the depths of the stall. By the time he got there, Sarah had managed to get the horse inside and closed the doors.

He saw that she'd replaced the floor so it looked much as they'd found it. He could only imagine how it gutted her to ride away from the coins after just uncovering them.

There was too much white showing in the horse's eyes and his movements were skittish and excited, but Sarah had a magical way with the animal and he calmed under the influence of her soothing voice. "Find anything warm that you can. Saddle blankets, whatever," she said.

He took out his flashlight but searched in near darkness, coming across a couple of mildew-smelling wool blankets stacked in another stall and a length of rope, which he took along for good measure. As Sarah finished tightening the saddle cinch and slipping on the bridle, he stuffed what he could in the saddlebags. He'd carry the rest.

"Okay, let's go," she whispered, switching off her light.

Nate opened both halves of the door and Sarah led the horse out of the stall. He closed the door behind them. Soft flakes fell on his face as he looked up at Sarah, who had mounted Skipjack. "He'll have to carry us both," he said.

"He can do it."

Nate settled himself behind Sarah, one of the blankets rolled and stuffed between them. This was her horse, her stomping ground. He just hoped there was a way out of the pasture that didn't go past the front of the house or they'd be dead meat.

Sarah headed across the back of the pasture toward the darker shapes of the trees, the only noises the creaking of the saddle, the crunch of the horse's hooves in the snow and the wind still blowing through the branches. Sarah seemed to be giving Skipjack his head as he picked his way through the foliage. The snow wasn't as deep under the cover of the trees, and the horse sped up under Sarah's quiet urging.

"Is there a gate back here?" Nate asked, leaning close

to speak softly. Her hair, smelling like cold, fresh hay, brushed his face. He had one hand around her waist, the other still supported by the sling, and her firm body rolled with the gait of the horse. For the first time in a while, he allowed himself a moment to think they might make it out of this mess, after all.

And then he remembered the man standing outside the house, pointing a gun, waiting. Would that man figure out no one had been in the house? Would he notice all the tracks between the house and the barn and would he then find the stall and the tracks leading away from it and toward the trees?

"Yes, there's a gate," she said. "And then there's a couple of miles of downhill terrain to a piece of land Dad bought years ago. There's a river and a fishing cabin on it…. It's abandoned, but it'll give us a place to wait out the rest of the night."

He didn't want to scare her any more than he had to, but stopping seemed a poor idea. "There was a man with a gun at the house," he said.

"What!" She turned her head briefly to look at him. "You're just now telling me?"

"This is the first opportunity I've had. He was waiting for one or both of us to run out the door. I can't believe he won't figure out where we've gone and how we left. Let's just keep riding until we find a phone or an occupied house or something."

"I can't," she said.

"What do you mean?"

Her voice tightened as she dashed words over her shoulder toward him. "Are you forgetting my mother?"

"No, but—"

"But nothing. You want to call the cops. If I get involved

with them, I'll never get the coins if they're still there to get, and I'll never save my mother in time."

"Even if the coins remain undiscovered, the house is on fire. Someone will call the fire department. By tomorrow, the place will be crawling with investigators."

"Maybe not. The place is pretty remote, no near neighbors, and in this weather, well, I have to try, don't you see? This isn't open to debate, Nate."

"Listen to me. If the coins are gone, it means Bellows or his buddies took them. Your mother will be okay."

"Maybe. But I can't bank on them finding the coins. I have to get my hands on some kind of vehicle that can handle cross-country and go back as soon as I can. Nothing has changed."

"That means a snowmobile."

"Yeah, it does, and I can't do that until daylight. I have to stay away from any involvement with the police until I have the luxury of time to explain all of this. You know that."

He swallowed any further comment. It went against his nature to avoid the law, but he could see her point.

"If you want me to let you off somewhere near other houses, just say so and I will. But don't go to the police, please—not until you hear from me that Mom is safe."

"I'll stay with you," he said. "I told you I would help and I will."

She nodded briskly.

They fell silent as the trees began to thin out and a sliver of moon actually showed now and then through the clouds. "The fence is up ahead," Sarah said, "and then the easiest way to travel the next half mile or so is to stick close to the highway. I don't know if we should do that."

"The arsonist had a snowmobile," Nate said. "He probably isn't using roads."

A few minutes later, Nate caught sight of the fence. When Skipjack got close enough to the gate, they both dismounted to open it. This was no easy task, thanks to the drifts of deeper snow pinning it closed. It took both of them digging with their hands to get enough clearance for the horse to pass. No way could they close it again, and so they left it open.

Beneath Nate's grip, Sarah's slim body shivered as they moved forward. Nate carefully unfurled a little of the wool blanket and draped it around her shoulders, making something of an impromptu hood to protect her head, as well. His own was still bare, and he missed his old Stetson with a passion.

"Thanks," she said, her voice a little muffled now by the blanket. He laid his cheek against the back of her head and murmured acknowledgment he doubted she heard.

A few minutes later, they came across the road Sarah had mentioned, a winding stretch of white the width of two lanes, closely banked on either side by dense forest, all leading downhill. For a while, they rode alongside it, but then they saw approaching headlights and Sarah guided Skipjack toward the trees again, where they would hopefully blend into the deep shadows.

"I felt like a sitting duck out there," Sarah said as an older truck slowly passed them by, the clinking noise of the chains on its tires diminishing as its taillights disappeared around a bend. "It'll take a little longer, but we're going to stay off the road."

Nate gripped her around the waist a little tighter. "You're behind the wheel."

An hour later, when Nate judged it to be near two o'clock in the morning, Sarah stopped the horse. The moon had broken through even more, and it reflected off the small river that glimmered through the trees at the bottom of the shallow glen before them. She urged Skipjack forward and the horse found footing on the snowy path leading down toward the water.

"There's the fishing cabin," Sarah said at last, once more pulling the horse to a stop. It was impossible to make out the details of the tiny structure through the snow and in the poor light, but what he did see wasn't particularly encouraging. On the other hand, it had a roof and seemed to have only one door, so as a place to guard, it had the house and barn beat to hell.

He slid off Skipjack's back first, then reached up to help Sarah dismount. Still half shrouded in the blanket, she landed right in front of him, and for a second, she seemed to sag. He leaned down and kissed her forehead a few times, holding her against his chest, the blanket slipping from her head, her hair a soft cloud against his cheek.

"You can do better than that," she said softly, turning her face up to his.

It was surreal to kiss her right then as the wind teased snow to fall from the overhead branches and the horse breathed warm air down their necks. He closed his eyes as their lips met, and the kiss he'd planned, a short one they could improve upon when they weren't cold and bleeding and wet, escalated in the first second until he'd parted her lips with his tongue and explored every inch of her tantalizing mouth. She responded with equal gusto until the horse tossed his head, rattling his bridle, snorting into the cold air and reminding them where they were and what still had to be accomplished.

"He's worse than an overbearing parent," Sarah whispered as they smiled at each other. She turned to face the horse. "Okay, big fella, let's get your saddle off." Nate reluctantly released his grip on her and came away with the blanket.

"There's a lean-to and a small fenced corral over by the trees. We'll have to trust the fence is in good repair." She led Skipjack into the enclosure and relieved him of his saddle and bridle while Nate used the flashlight to examine the lean-to. He found an old stump under the cover, and embedded in the stump was a thing of beauty, a double-bitted hand ax, the kind used to chop kindling for a fire. He yanked it from the stump and shone the light on it.

"What did you find?" Sarah asked.

"An ax," he told her. "It's a little rusty, but it's sharp enough."

"Sharp enough for what?" she said.

"To use as a weapon if need be. Let's get in out of this cold."

The cabin's tiny porch was more of a covered step than anything else and the unlocked door opened inward to a small square room. As they shined the flashlights around the space, Nate saw a counter of sorts running along one wall complete with a sink and a small hand pump for water. A few shelves above the counter held scattered plates, cups and cooking utensils. There didn't seem to be any food and the nearby stove was the kind campers the world over used.

Two chairs flanked a small table situated beneath the rear window while a small wood-burning stove promised heat. A mattress on the floor of the farthest wall served as a bed. Nate tossed the blankets onto the mattress. As rustic as it all was, that bed looked like heaven to Nate, and he imagined Sarah had the same bone-weary response as he.

"Do you want me to build a fire?" he asked her.

"No. It's too late for that. I just want to sleep. There's a lantern under the sink with all the fishing gear," Sarah said, the beam of her flashlight considerably dimmer than it had been a couple of hours earlier. She found the lantern and they lit it with difficulty with matches from a box someone had left on the table.

"Keep the light turned low and on the floor," Nate cautioned as he hooked one of the chairs and propped it under the doorknob to block access. "No need to advertise we're here." He was glad she'd refused a fire, as the smoke from the chimney would be as telling as a light.

"I agree," she said, unzipping her jacket. She produced Mike's notebook and handed it to him. "Maybe that will do for a little light reading."

They stared at each other for a few moments, then, in unspoken agreement, sank down on the mattress and pulled off their boots. Sarah had to help Nate accomplish this and he smiled as he watched her.

"I could get used to being babied this way," he said as he raised his good arm. She settled in against him, both with their backs against the wall. He'd set the ax on the floor beside the mattress, where he could reach it if need be.

"So, this is your dad's fishing cabin. It must be hard coming here tonight after all that happened today."

She nodded, her eyes growing soft. "His death has kind of been pushed to a back burner because of everything else that's happened. In some ways it's hard to believe he's gone, that he won't come bursting in here with a string of fish."

"I wish he could," Nate said. "I'm starving."

"I know. Me, too."

"Wait a second," he said, shaking his head as he reached into the big coat's pockets and withdrew two small apples. He handed one to Sarah.

"Where did you get these?" she asked and took a bite.

"From the barrel outside of Skipjack's stall. I don't know if they're any good—I grabbed a couple when I was looking for blankets."

"It's delicious," Sarah said, happily munching away.

Nate took a bite of his own. The apple wasn't great, but nothing had ever tasted better, and he wished he'd taken time to gather a few more. They ate in silence for a while, savoring the juicy fruit. "Did you come here often when you were a kid?" he asked.

She swallowed and wiped her chin with her fingers. "Off and on. I wasn't much for fishing, but I loved exploring the riverbank. We had a cocker spaniel named Rosie. She was a swimming fool."

"I like dogs," Nate said.

"Do you have one now?"

"Two. A black Lab and a little scruffy white thing that showed up one day. The Lab likes to go horseback riding with me, but he's a terror in the river, so I can't take him when I go fishing. He scares all the fish away."

"You live somewhere you can have horses?"

He smiled at the enthusiasm he could hear in her voice. "Sure. I have a few acres that border a national preserve. I've got horses, some cattle, a pregnant goat and a handful of chickens. I've also got coyotes and rattlesnakes."

"Sounds like heaven, except for the snakes."

"It is. I take it you've been living in a city."

She polished off her apple. "Yes, but my heart is in the country. It tore me apart to leave the ranch, but at least I had plans to work with animals. Those dreams got me through the marriage and Johnny's death, the meaningless jobs, everything. And then Mom needed the money, and, well…what else could I do but help her?"

"You have money now," Nate said gently. "Thanks to your father, you can go to the best college in the country and become a world-class veterinarian."

She nodded as she took his apple core and laid it on the floor beside her own. He produced a red bandanna from his pocket and they both wiped their hands dry. "Yeah, thanks to Dad."

They were quiet for a minute, then Nate asked a question. "Do you know where you can get a snowmobile in the morning?"

"I think so. Fred and Emma Crawley live a mile or so from here. They used to let me use theirs. If they remember me, I'm sure I can borrow it."

He leaned his head against hers. "They'll remember you."

She pulled away a little and stared up at him. "You sound so sure of it."

"Well, who could forget you?"

She was quiet for a second and he wondered what was going on inside her head, then she murmured, "They haven't actually seen me since I was seventeen."

"When you ran off with an older guy—a cop, to boot. Probably makes you infamous in a small place like this."

"Probably," she whispered, settling against him again. "As long as my mother makes it out of this alive—"

"I'm hoping you and I make it out alive," Nate interrupted.

Again she pulled away to look at him. "That goes without saying. But Mom—"

"—got you into this mess," Nate said. "I hope she's worth what you're risking."

"She's my mother," Sarah said with a note of finality in her voice.

"I understand that," Nate said.

She looked down at her lap. "Do you?" she murmured.

Nate didn't respond. He was glad when she leaned against him again, but it was obvious it was more for comfort and warmth than closeness, and he guessed he'd earned that from her. He closed his own eyes but his mind raced with the images and impressions of the past few hours. Now, in the relative safety and quiet of this remote cabin, every thought revolved around the woman next to him.

She was such an enigma to him. There were parts of her so competent and brazen that she made him shudder in despair that she would do something incredibly dangerous—like try to negotiate with the thug she'd described, Bellows. But there was also something about her that suggested she was no fool when it came to self-preservation. And what about that loyal streak of hers, and for a mother who seemed to have done little to earn it? Nate's own parents were good, upstanding people who had never told a single lie that he knew of. That was the way he'd been raised, too.

How could he take credit for that? His folks had made choices that spared him having to choose between lying to a stranger and forsaking one of them. They had never asked for help in a life-and-death situation, and if they had, what would he have done to ensure their safety?

Anything. He would have done whatever it took. In Sarah's shoes, he would do the same.

He opened his eyes, intent on telling her this, but she'd grown heavier against him, her breathing softer and more steady. He twisted his head and looked down at her, admiring the sweep of dark lashes against her cheeks and the supple peachy glow of her lips. While part of him ached to wake her with a juicy kiss, another part was content to watch her. Had he ever felt this way before?

And what would Mike have made of this instant attraction between his daughter and Nate? Mike...almost forgotten in the rush to save his daughter and his ex-wife.

With thoughts of Mike came equally disquieting ones of Alex. Why hadn't he shown up in Shatterhorn? Had he had to make an emergency landing somewhere else?

If he had, Nate was sure one of the first things he would do was find a phone and try to make contact. However, Nate's phone was history, so any calls would appear to go unanswered and that would concern Alex. Hopefully his friend would call home and Jessica could explain that they'd spoken.

With any luck, he and Alex would soon be downing a beer together and recounting their individual adventures. While Nate looked forward to that, he dreaded the thought of trying to explain Mike's murder.

Which reminded Nate of Mike's notebook that he'd tucked beside his leg. He picked it up now, working it free from the rubber bands, holding it turned to the lantern light. At first he wasn't sure if it was fatigue or poor lighting, but nothing made a lot of sense. Gradually, though, he was able to see that it was part personal diary, part schedules and impressions of interviews and stakeouts, part musings that seemed to be his way of assimilating information. Sometimes Mike had folded a cut-out newspaper article within the pages, or quoted from an article or perhaps something he heard on the radio. It appeared one page had been torn out, as the jagged edge sticking out of the binding attested. And he'd made a list. For an appliance salesman, Mike showed signs of latent detective skills.

The first word on the list was *Fireworks*. The second was *Pearl*. Nate knew that had been the mall shooter's last word. But seeing it here and followed by the date December 7, with the notation of Pearl Harbor Day right after it, startled Nate.

The mall shooting had happened on Labor Day. Mike also mentioned a Veterans Day incident at a library in Arlington, Virginia, five dead. The Hawaii shooting had happened on Pearl Harbor Day. Was it possible the dying man's last word had not referred to a gem taken from a mollusk but the holiday commemorating the attack on Pearl Harbor?

But how could that sorry excuse for the kid at the mall have known anything about shootings that would take place several months down the road?

Nate flipped back a page and found an article about a July Fourth incident. Two months before the mall shooting, a gunman had slain two victims during a fireworks display in the middle of Iowa. The gunman had been killed when the crowd finally figured out that not all the explosions and shouting were coming from enthralled onlookers and gone after him. Nate vaguely remembered reading about it. He couldn't remember if any foreign group had taken credit for it.

The second-to-last word on the list was *Washington*. *Washington*. Sarah had said her father went on and on about it, growing frustrated with her when she kept assuming he was talking about where she used to live. What if he was talking about the city in a different context?

Memorial was the last word. Did that mean the Washington Memorial? Had he meant the *Washington Monument?* Was it possible terrorists were targeting American national holidays? Was that what Mike had thought? Was that why he'd been hounding the editor of the paper and the only politician he knew, the mayor of a small town who had smothered them in accolades after the mall shooting? Had Mike been trying to enlist their aid in reaching a broader audience?

The last few pages held notes on People's Liberation, all written in tiny script and all crossed out with a scribbled *NO!* across the top. And on the very last page that had been used was the number twenty-eight, circled in red ink.

The words began to swim before Nate's eyes and he closed the book. Maybe if he slept for a few minutes, his head would clear enough that he could figure out exactly what Mike had been trying to say. He turned off the lantern and adjusted the blankets to cover Sarah's feet and his own shoulders, then, leaning his head against her, closed his eyes.

He awoke standing beside Sarah. She was dressed in a blue skirt, her hair curled and bouncy. Her white blouse was covered with little red and black flowers that gradually morphed into the suits of a deck of cards—diamonds, hearts, spades and clubs. She pulled on his hand, yanking him to a booth of sorts. She pointed at a pearl necklace.

They were suddenly inside a mall and the place was crowded with tiny children, preschoolers, really, running everywhere, laughing, but Nate felt an all-pervading weight of anxiety. He had to get Sarah away from that booth, which was suddenly crawling with babies who were falling to the floor. He and Sarah each started grabbing the infants, but there were too many to save them all.

Booming gunfire stopped everything and Nate's arm exploded. He was alone except for Sarah lying at his feet, her blouse red now. He knelt beside her and she opened her eyes. "Save my mother, Nate," she whispered. "Nate, Nate…"

He sobbed as she disappeared into smoke. His shoulder ached. He groaned and Sarah said, "Nate? Are you okay? Wake up."

His eyes flew open to face the dark room. "I'm awake," he said at last.

She gently rolled him over. All he could see of her was the slightly lighter shade of her face and the glistening of the whites of her eyes.

"You were having a nightmare," she said, smoothing his hair away from his brow.

He had nightmares almost every night. The only difference with this one was the fact Sarah had been part of it. If he was honest with himself, she'd been the center of it, a focus for his fears, eclipsing even the children.

"Are you okay now?" she added.

He took a couple of shallow breaths, then caught her hand and brought her fingers to his lips. She drew her hand away and he winced inside, but the interruption in physical contact was brief. She lay down beside him and put her arms around him as though he was a scared little kid. No one had done that since he was ten years old; he was used to being the strong one who protected, not the other way around.

The feel of her body pressed against his began to get through the nightmare hangover and arouse him in all the predictable ways. When she tenderly kissed his lips, he closed his eyes and hoped she'd never stop.

She kissed him a dozen times, all over the face, his eyelids, his cheeks, his nose and ears, all sweet, comforting kisses that he found anything but comforting. The next time her lips landed on his, he opened his mouth and that was like throwing gasoline on a fire. He longed to make love to her.

As though she'd read his mind, she unzipped his jacket and unbuttoned his shirt, doing both slowly, driving him mad as her fingertips grazed his skin. Although she was incredibly careful not to touch his left arm, she touched almost every other place she could reach, her strokes light and sexy and urgent, her kisses on his neck and chest sensuous, and as they traveled down his stomach toward his waist, he almost lost it.

He pulled her back up so he could claim her lips once again, knowing if she even fiddled with the buttons of his fly he'd stand no chance of making this last. Limited by the fact he could use only one hand, he made up for it with his mouth, sucking on her earlobe, licking her throat. Her coat and sweater were obstacles and he tugged on them, the need to feel her bare skin invading every organ in his body.

"Take them off," he whispered and she sat up. When she lay back down, she was naked from the waist up, her breasts soft alluring orbs, the nipples hard beneath his touch. She moaned deep in her throat when he put his mouth to one and fondled the other. He would have given anything for light enough to see her as well as feel her.

"Do you have something?" she asked, her voice breathless.

His hand traveled under her low-cut jeans, her heat and warmth and suppleness affecting him like a drug. "Have what?" he managed to say.

"Protection. A condom?"

"No," he said, burying his face in her hair. "Do you?"

"No," she whispered.

He couldn't get enough of her. He would have sucked her into his lungs if it was possible, tasted every little bit of her.

But something had changed, and it finally got through to him. His poor brain was so addled by her that it took a second to connect her request with her withdrawal.

He held her head under his chin and kissed her hair.

"I have to have protection," she whispered. "I can't have sex without it. I mean, I want to have children someday, but not like this. I just can't risk pregnancy."

"It's okay," he assured her. "You're right."

"And you were so recently engaged to someone else."

"And you were going to shoot me just a few short hours ago. Don't forget that." Her soft chuckle made him smile in the dark. "All of this is true, but it doesn't change the fact that I want you so much it hurts," he murmured.

She raised his hand to her mouth and kissed his fingers.

"It's going to be light soon. I'm going to try to get a little more sleep."

Holding her was exquisite torture, but that was okay. Her soft, fragrant body pressed up against him would keep him wide-awake all night. He should never have allowed himself to go to sleep in the first place—it wouldn't pay to forget the image of their adversary poised outside the house ready to pick them off when they tried to escape a fire.

And there was another image he hadn't told Sarah about, because there wasn't much they could do about it. Often, on the ride across the pasture, he'd glanced behind them, afraid they were being followed. He'd never seen anyone, but once the sky lightened, it would reveal the path the horse had left in the snow. For all intents and purposes, they might as well have sprinkled fluorescent bread crumbs in their wake. And down here with the river on one side and a hill on the other, they were as good as trapped.

Chapter Nine

Sarah woke up with a start. Morning had come, and soft light filtered through the dirty, cracked windows of the cabin. She twisted her arm up to look at her watch and saw it was almost 8:00 a.m. She'd overslept.

"Wake up," she told Nate as she extricated herself from beneath his arm. She grabbed her sweater and jacket from where she'd discarded them the night before, aware of Nate's gray gaze watching her dress. She grabbed her boots and pulled them on, then got to her feet.

"Hurry up," she said, moving to the sink, where she pumped ice-cold water into her hands and splashed it on her face. She rinsed out her mouth with more of the same, glanced at Nate and found him slowly buttoning his shirt. She knew it would be hard for him to tug on his boots with the injured arm, but he'd make it.

"I'll go saddle Skipjack," she said and moved the chair to let herself outside the cabin, where she paused for a second as she closed the door. It was a relief to get away from Nate. She hadn't even been able to meet his gaze. She'd been embarrassed by recalling overwhelming intimacy after such a short time knowing one another and clearly remembered rattling on about a baby—something she hadn't thought about in years and something a woman shouldn't start talking about with a man she barely knew.

It was all like a bad dream. Well, maybe not all of it. There was no denying the passion, no denying the desire…and no denying her empathy for his pain.

She just really didn't want to know what he thought about her this morning.

But more important, why had she let down her guard last night and told him so much about her mother's predicament? Who was to say he wouldn't start arguing with her again about going to the police? There wasn't time for a bunch of maneuvering. She had to get back to the house, get the silver and drive to Reno.

Maybe she should leave him here and go by herself. Why had she even woken him up?

Skipjack came to her call as she let herself into the corral. She picked up his bridle from where she'd stowed it the night before and slipped it over his head, then lifted the saddle and settled it atop the saddle blanket. As she flipped the stirrup up to fasten the cinch, something glinted in the rocks downstream. She quickly looked away.

"Let's see that foot, sweetie," she crooned to the horse. She bent down to pick up his foreleg and pretended to study his shoe while she peered downstream. Then she put Skipjack's leg down and wound his reins around the fence. "I'll be right back," she said with a pat to his flank. She let herself out the gate and casually walked to the cabin.

Nate was standing with his back to her at the sink. At the sound of the door, he turned, water glistening on his stubbled jaw, looking twice as worn-out and three times as sexy as he had the day before. "What's wrong?" he snapped after a searching look at her face.

"Someone is out there," she said.

Drying his face with a towel, he started to look out the window, but she stopped him. "Don't—he'll see you. He's downstream, hiding among some rocks. I saw the flash of something like binoculars."

"Could it be a neighbor or someone coming to use the cabin?"

"No. The land is posted, but beyond that factor, the Crawleys are the nearest neighbors and they're eighty years old. I don't think they're running around spying on people the morning after a snowstorm."

"Do you think whoever it is knows you're onto him?"

"I don't think so. I tried to act like nothing was wrong. Nate, I have a plan."

He looked at her and she could tell that he wasn't expecting much. "I don't have time for an argument, so just hear me out," she said. "We need to get this guy off our back once and for all. So, here's what we're going to do. I'm going to go out there again and piddle around while you sneak out the window. If you use the trees for cover, you should be able to circle around and come at him from the other direction. Then you hit him or something, we tie him up, take his snowmobile and go get the coins to save my mother."

Nate's eyebrows shot up his forehead. "Honestly, Sarah, are you forgetting that this person is probably the same one who spent most of yesterday afternoon and evening trying to kill you?"

"He could have shot me while I was saddling the horse," she said as she gripped the doorknob. "Maybe all along he was just trying to get our attention so he could steal the coins."

"Talk about being a sitting duck. I am not going to let you use yourself as bait—"

"I'm depending on you," she interrupted and, without waiting for him to disagree more adamantly, let herself back outside. She heard him swear as she moved off the porch.

It was amazingly difficult to act natural knowing someone was watching. She did her best to look busy as she once again entered the corral and sat on her heels, running her hands up and down Skipjack's front leg as a diversion. This time when she dared a glance, she didn't see any reflection near the rocks and her heart skipped up her throat. Had he moved? Or had she been mistaken? She'd been so sure, but now she didn't know.

She left the corral again and walked toward the river as though admiring the view, glancing at her watch now and again. If she had been mistaken about someone being out here, she and Nate were now wasting time better spent getting to the Crawley place and borrowing a snowmobile.

She wanted to look around for Nate but kept her back to the rocks and the trees. She heard footsteps crunching the snow and realized Nate had reached the same conclusion. She turned to talk to him.

But it wasn't Nate. Instead she found herself looking at a man dressed in gray-and-white camouflage gear with a black ski mask covering most of his face. A pair of green binoculars dangled around his neck and he carried a revolver. That gun was currently aimed at her heart.

"Are you Bellows or one of his henchmen?" she asked, resisting the urge to scan behind him for some sign of Nate.

"Where is he?" the man asked. His voice sounded young and wired.

"Who? Bellows?"

"No, the guy you were with. Matthews."

"He left," she said. "He's off calling the cops."

"I don't think so," the man said. "There are tracks into this place but none out." He cocked the gun, advanced a few steps and repeated, "Where is he?" The tip of the gun inched up to Sarah's forehead.

"Hey," she said. "If you hurt me or him, you'll never find the money."

"What money?"

He didn't know about the coins? "Who sent you?" she asked. "Who are you?"

"Listen, lady, you're going to end up floating facedown in the river in about two seconds if you don't tell me where Matthews is."

"What do you want with him? I'm the one who can help you."

He finished closing the distance between them, grabbed her arm with a viselike grip and propelled her toward the cabin. "Call for him," he said.

"No."

The tip of the barrel pressed against her throat. She could feel her pulse beating against the metal. "Call for him."

Where is Nate?

The gun pressed harder.

She was shaking so hard it was difficult to stand. Surely Nate had left the cabin. Surely he knew what was going on. But where was he?

"One last time," the man hissed in her ear. "Call for Matthews to come out of the cabin. Tell him you need help."

"He'll see you through the window," she said. "He won't come out here."

"Then we'll make him." The man's iron grip slid up to her neck, but before he could tighten his grasp, Sarah stomped on his foot and took off. She knew she'd pay for this action with a bullet in the back, but she had to try. She got an arm's length away before he grabbed her by the hair and yanked her back, shoving her to the ground in the process. He pointed the gun at her. She saw his mouth open through the gap in his ski mask and her heart stopped beating.

No words left his lips. Instead he made a sound as if all the air had been pushed from his lungs. He fell forward onto Sarah, pinning her legs beneath his torso. Sarah found herself staring at a hatchet buried in the brute's back.

She began screaming and couldn't stop. Nate was suddenly there and he pulled her out from under the man. She shielded her eyes by burying her face in his jacket and he led her to the corral, where he gently pushed her onto the stump once used to chop kindling.

"I'll be right back," he said and returned to the man on the ground. She watched as he sat on his haunches and felt for a pulse, then closed her eyes as a wave of nausea rose up her throat. She got to her feet, wondering what they would do if the man was still alive. Common decency said they would have to go for help. But that meant Sarah's mother would perish.

"Is he dead?" she asked Nate as he returned to her.

"Yes. Are you all right?"

"I'll be fine. Did you find his snowmobile?"

"Yeah, it's back in the trees. Is that Bellows?"

"I didn't see his face. He sounded too young, though. And he wanted you, not me."

Nate's brow furrowed. "Me? Why would he want me?"

"I have no idea. He didn't seem to know anything about any money, either."

Nate shook his head. "This doesn't make sense. Are you up to looking at his face?"

"If I have to," she said and followed Nate back to the slain man. His head lay to one side, and Nate pulled up the ski mask. She saw a young guy in his early twenties, maybe late teens. She looked past the bloody bubbles around his lips and studied his features. "I kind of recognize him. Do you?"

Nate ran a hand through his dark hair. "He does look familiar but I don't know why. Damn it, I didn't want to kill him, but it was the only way to stop him before he shot you."

"You don't hear me complaining," Sarah said, turning away from the dead man. "Nate, we need to take the snowmobile and go get the coins."

"It's a one-seater. There are saddlebags, but two people won't fit."

"Then I have to go alone," Sarah said. A little while ago, that had seemed like a great idea, but now Sarah hated the thought of riding out of here without Nate.

"I could go instead of you," he said.

She averted her gaze from the dead man on the ground. "I'm the one who has to drive to Reno, and time is ticking away." She paused before adding, "This is my responsibility, Nate."

A tilt of his head said clearly that he understood what she meant. "And mine is to contact the law. I've just killed a man and then there's your father's murder to try to explain."

"I know you have to do what you feel is right and what's important to you. Tell the sheriff's department whatever you have to—just give me an hour or so to get the coins and get out of here."

"How are you going to do that?" he asked. "Your car may have been confiscated, but even if it hasn't, the snow is still too deep. The fire department could still be there, too. If a spark got to my truck, it might have blown up. The ranch could be a real disaster."

"I know. I don't know how I'm going to get to Reno, but somehow, I will."

"Sarah, there's something else. We have no way of knowing if this man is the one from last night."

She thought for a few seconds before speaking. "You wounded the one last night. Does this guy have any bullet holes?"

"I'll look."

"I have to go," she said.

"I know you do."

"And, Nate, when you talk to the cops, could you just not mention the coins, you know, for now?"

He stared down into her eyes. "I won't mention them, but when this is all over—"

"I'll sing like a canary," she promised. She gazed up into his eyes and gripped his uninjured arm. "Nate, I'm scared. This guy didn't know about the coins or give a hoot about me. He wanted you."

Nate nodded. "It takes a little getting used to, doesn't it? But if it is the same guy from yesterday then Bellows had nothing to do with any of this. That's good news for you and your mother. Pay off the debt and walk away."

"It's not me I'm thinking of," Sarah said. "It's you. He was ready to kill me to get to you. He may not be alone. Be careful."

"I will. But you be careful, too. Just because this guy today was after me doesn't mean last night wasn't all about you."

She nodded and glanced at her watch. "Take Skipjack," she said. "There's a large-animal veterinarian on the east edge of town that Dad has used for years. I'm pretty sure they'll keep him for you."

He raised his right hand and cupped her chin. "I hate

letting you go off on your own. There's so much we have to finish."

"I know. The police and—"

"That's not what I meant," he said.

She swallowed a lump and blinked rapidly. "Just be careful," she repeated.

He leaned over and claimed her lips, and Sarah was shocked to discover in that instant leaving him was the hardest thing she'd done yet. There had been so much fear lately, so much loss, and this felt like another. Would she ever see him again? He kissed her one more time, lightly, then whispered against her lips, "Go now."

Sarah sucked back tears as she turned away and ran off into the trees.

As DISTASTEFUL AS it was, Nate pulled off the dead man's ski mask and gloves and searched for a sign of a gunshot wound inflicted a mere twelve hours earlier. Then he unzipped his jacket and patted him down. He found no identification, no bloody bandages or injuries, although if he'd been shot in the back the night before, it sure wouldn't show now. The ax had made a real mess of things, and for a moment Nate thought about that split-second decision to launch the ax rather than take the time to try to run up to him unheard and hit him over the head.

It hadn't really been a hard decision to make. It was this guy or Sarah, and she'd won. He suspected she would win every contest in his head. He heard the snowmobile and looked up the slope in time to see her erupt from the trees and disappear over the lip of the cliff.

He collected a dozen rocks from the riverbed, carrying them back up to the body, then retrieved a blanket from the mattress inside the cabin. His plan was to cover the body with the blanket and secure it with rocks. Lying on the snow as it was, the body should be pretty well preserved until the police arrived.

Before he did this, he studied the guy's profile one more time, and again, there was something about him that looked a little familiar. Something about the cheekbones and the jaw. Something—but nothing definite.

Once he climbed on Skipjack's back, he realized he wasn't sure the quickest way to anywhere—he was totally turned around—but there was a road up there somewhere. If he could find that, he could find people, help, a phone.

And then he could face the music for killing a man and try to explain what had happened at Mike's house yesterday.

Would he ever see Sarah again? Nate had a gut feeling that the guy he'd just killed had not been the same one he'd shot the day before. Like he'd told Sarah, it was possible there were two agendas at work, possible that Sarah was walking into a death trap and there wasn't a thing he could do about it.

Or could he?

SARAH HADN'T KNOWN exactly what to expect at the ranch. Firemen, probably, maybe the police. It was a long shot that she could sneak in there and steal her own coins out from under them, so she approached warily, parking the snowmobile by Skipjack's stall and entering the barn as quietly as she could.

To her great relief, the stall looked just as she'd left it. She took a detour to the front of the barn, where she found the door wide open and the cold, thin wind tunneling inside. Moving in the shadows to avoid being seen from outside, she made her way to a vantage point from which she could see the house. It took her a second to believe her eyes. There wasn't a soul around or any sign that anyone had been. With the exception of partially burned wood siding, nothing looked any different than it had hours before. Had the gunman extinguished it himself or had the house refused to burn? She blinked a couple of times but in the end decided to accept it as a stroke of luck and hurried back to the stall.

She quickly moved the straw bedding and then shoveled up the dirt in the corner. The cans were right where they were supposed to be, and as she hooked the first one with her fingers, she glanced at her watch. She had four hours to get the coins and herself to Reno. She couldn't drive her car, she couldn't take the snowmobile all that way and she couldn't rent a car. As she moved the coins from the cans into the saddlebags, she found herself close to giggling. *Heck, I could buy a car.* She could buy a fleet of cars as long as no one needed to see a license or any identification.

She did the math in her head to come up with what her mother needed. The value of the coins far exceeded their actual weight because of their mint condition—she wasn't sure how to figure it all out, but at this point, she would be happy to fork over too much if it meant ending this nightmare.

Which begged the question, how did she assure her mother didn't get herself back into the same old mess a week or a month or a year from now? She would find out that Sarah had inherited everything from Mike, and as soon as she did, little by little she would eat it all up in her wild gambling sprees. Sooner or later, the money would end up in the pockets of Poulter or Bellows or others of their ilk, and it galled Sarah to death. Her father had sat on most of the coins his entire adult life; he hadn't kept up the ranch or bought himself new cars, nothing, just let the coins sit in their cans and then left them to Sarah, who would now need to figure out a way to assure they did some actual good in the world.

Talk about problems for another day. Right now she had to get into Shatterhorn and beg, steal or borrow a car. Three and a half hours…

Because there were still several cans of coins in the underground vault, she had to take the time to put the stall back together again, working up a sweat despite the cold temperature. A weak sun came out as she rode off, and she squinted at the brilliance as the light reflected off the snow. A pair of goggles hung from the handlebars, but they had to have belonged to the man Nate killed and Sarah didn't want them touching her face. As it was, her face was soon so cold she couldn't feel her lips or her nose.

She looked back once as she crossed the pasture, then concentrated on driving, trying in the back of her mind to figure out how she should go about the next step, her hands half-frozen, her hair whipping about her shoulders.

She still had friends from high school living in Shatterhorn; maybe one of them could loan her a car. But how did she show up on their doorstep after eleven years' absence and ask without delivering a long explanation she didn't have the time for? For that matter, where did they currently live and how did she get to their houses while lugging around almost a hundred pounds of silver coins?

Nor, Sarah admitted, did she want any of them knowing her mother still gambled. Diana Donovan's antics had been the talk of the town once, and once was enough.

Sarah had been driving beside the highway for the past mile or so. The road itself had been plowed and traffic was light. A short time later, the snowmobile belched its first sputter. She was still a half a mile from Shatterhorn. A couple of hundred feet more and it became clear the machine was about out of gas. She managed to guide it behind a spur of old fence before its last gasping moment, hoping to hide it from sight, but what did she do now?

Caught in a web of indecision and rising panic, she started stuffing the rolled coins into her pockets, knowing it was hopeless, not knowing what else she could do. Her watch kept catching the reflection of the sun, twinkling at her, taunting her.

She heard the sound of a car approaching and ducked her head, unsure if Nate had had time to coax the police into starting their investigation, only knowing she didn't want to get involved in any part of that until there was no other choice. She caught the blurred shape of a dark blue truck passing her by, then looked over her shoulder to witness it make a screeching U-turn before stopping several feet away. Nate leaned across the front seat and opened the passenger door. "Need a ride?"

She scrambled to climb inside. "What are you doing here?"

"I'm driving you to Reno if you managed to get the coins. Did you?"

"Yes. Whoever started the fire must have put it out. The house shows where it burned and the barn door was open as though someone looked around in there, too, but that's it. Maybe they didn't want authorities snooping around prematurely. Now that you've gone to the police—"

"I haven't talked to them yet," he said. "I was on my way out to the ranch when I caught a glimpse of you behind that fence."

"That's where the snowmobile is. I ran out of gas. Where's my horse?"

"At the vet. They said they'll board him until you come for him." As he told her this, he positioned the truck as close to the side of the road as he could, and together, they transferred the coins from the attached saddlebags and

Sarah's pockets, piling the rolls in a cardboard box in the backseat. Sarah could see Nate was favoring his arm and wondered how much it still hurt.

At last he made another U-turn and they took off.

She stared at him for several seconds before finally speaking. "Why aren't you spilling your guts to the cops?"

He spared her a quick glance as he merged onto a major highway leading west toward Reno. "What's the rush?" he asked.

She studied his strong profile for a moment before shaking her head. "Well, let's see. A, there are two dead men, and B, you're a deputy sheriff who has, until this minute, seemed hell-bent on following the rules."

"I believe I told you I knew how to think outside the box," he said, but there was something else in his voice that caught her attention. Exactly what it was, she wasn't sure.

"Yeah, but, Nate, think about it. This could get you in a heap of trouble," she added.

"You, too," he said.

"I'm used to trouble. I get the feeling you're not."

The look he flashed her this time was more intense. "Mike is dead and can't be brought back to life no matter when law enforcement gets into the act. The same goes for our visitor this morning. But your situation is immediate and dangerous and I don't want you doing it alone."

"You keep forgetting someone showed up this morning intent on killing you. Not me—you," she said.

"I haven't forgotten. In fact, I finally figured out who it was."

"Are you going to tell me?"

He flashed her a grim smile. "I thought you'd never ask."

Chapter Ten

"It's Peter Jacks," Nate said.

Sarah felt like slapping her forehead. "I didn't really recognize him. I should have, but I didn't."

"People look different when they're dead. Besides, it's been several years since you saw him, right?"

"Over ten. He was just a kid I babysat occasionally. He gave no indication he recognized me, either. How did you figure out who he was?"

"He looked familiar to me. I talked myself into a few minutes of internet use while I was renting the truck. I found a photograph taken of Thomas's family leaving his funeral, and there, front and center, was his older brother, Peter."

"So he wanted to kill you for, what, revenge? Because you were at the mall when his brother went berserk? But you didn't kill Thomas. He killed himself. Why go after you?"

"I'm not sure," Nate admitted. He hadn't thought it all the way through yet.

"Does this mean he killed my father, too?"

"I don't know."

"How would Peter Jacks know you were in Nevada unless my father told him?"

"He wouldn't."

"No, and my father looked as though he was caught coming home or leaving his house, not like he'd been in the middle of a heart-to-heart chat with Peter." She gestured at the road ahead and added, "Can't you go any faster?"

"Sure I can," he said and sped up. The nervous energy emanating from Sarah permeated the cab.

"Did you find a gunshot wound on Peter's body?" she asked.

"No," Nate said. "But that doesn't mean there wasn't one. I could hardly strip him." The truth was, Nate had been happy to have an explanation for the morning's disaster, but now he saw that Sarah made some valid points. "After we talk to the Shatterhorn police, I want to arrange to see a couple of other people. Your dad's notebook mentioned conversations but didn't really specify content. Maybe the people he spoke with will remember what it was about. And maybe one of them will know if there was contact between your dad and the Jacks family."

"You may not be able to arrest anyone in Nevada, but you still approach things as the cop you are," she said. "Do you think they're involved with Dad's murder?"

Nate kept his eyes on the road ahead. "Impossible to say. Until we know for sure, we have to assume the people who have your mother were at your father's house yesterday, busily trying to kill us. We'd better concentrate on keeping a few steps ahead of this guy when we get to Reno. How are you supposed to deliver the money?"

"He gave me a phone number to call before three o'clock. He said he'll tell me where he stashed my mother and we'll make an exchange."

Nate glanced at the dashboard clock. They were about twenty miles from Reno and it was after one. "We have to make time to hit a coin dealer first. You can't just shovel out silver coins in front of Bellows."

"I'll have to call him first and make sure I know exactly how much Mom owes him. Then I'll sell enough coins to meet that debt. I wonder if one dealer will have enough cash?"

"I guess we'll find out. I sure hate the idea of these thugs getting away with it."

"I know you do," she said with a swift glance Nate caught out of the corner of his eye. "But that's exactly what's going to happen. I thought you were okay with this."

"I can agree with you but still not like it," he said.

She laughed softly. "Yeah, that's true."

A half hour later, they pulled into the almost empty parking lot of the first coin dealer they found. Nate was delighted, when they entered, to see the place was also a vendor for other merchandise, including prepaid cell phones. While Sarah talked with the dealer, he bought and activated a new phone, which would serve him fine until he could go back to his original carrier and replace the unit that had been shot out of his hand.

When he joined Sarah, he found her deep in negotiations with a balding Asian man who wore a jeweler's loupe and emitted a fierce aura of concentration. As the dealer carefully unpeeled the wrapper of a roll of silver dollars, Sarah looked up at Nate. "Where have you been?"

"I bought a phone. Why don't you go call Bellows and I'll stay here and watch over things."

Sarah took the phone, and as she walked away, Nate watched her dig in her hip pocket and withdraw a slip of paper that he assumed held the number she had to call. He had to force his gaze from her lithe figure, and when he did, he found the dealer looking at him with a speculative expression.

"She won't tell me where she got these coins," he said, nodding at the stack of rolls they'd deposited atop the cabinet.

"They're hers," Nate responded.

"You expect me to take your word for it?"

Nate wished he could open his wallet and show the guy his badge. "Have a little faith," he said instead.

"The deal is, there are a lot of coins here, and if they're all of this quality, we're talking a small fortune. You know I can't buy them without filing a CTR, right?"

"What's a CTR?"

"A currency transfer report. You know, the government's attempt to try to control money laundering." He rubbed his bald head. "I hope I have enough cash in the safe to purchase the whole lot. If not, I'll have to call my banker and arrange a transfer."

Nate propped his hands atop the cabinet and leaned forward. "We're in a bit of a hurry. How about you purchase all that you can and help us figure out how many more it'll take to come to a certain figure?"

"What figure?"

"We'll know when the lady returns. Just keep examining the ones you can afford to buy outright. We need to be out of here in fifteen minutes."

The man rubbed his head again. "Let me see what I can do."

As the dealer took out a pocket calculator, Nate went in search of Sarah. He found her standing outside with her back against the brick building, and as he approached, she clicked off the phone and looked up at him. There were tears in her eyes and Nate closed the distance between them as fast as possible.

"What's wrong?"

"Bellows put my mother on the phone. She was crying

so hard I couldn't understand much of what she said. I guess this maniac has been passing the time by detailing the ways he's going to torture her to teach us both a lesson if I don't show up."

"Were you able to ask her if she told them you were going up to see your father to ask for the money?"

"She was in no shape to think clearly. I didn't ask her much of anything." She hastily wiped a teardrop from her cheek and added, "We have an hour to get to the Silver Dollar Motel right outside of Carson City. We have to hurry."

"Are you kidding me? The Silver Dollar?"

"I know. Appropriate, isn't it?"

"Damn right poetic," he said. "How much money do we need?"

"Two hundred and twenty-eight thousand dollars."

"Let's go make this happen," Nate said and took her hand.

The dealer came up with all the money they needed to ransom Sarah's mother and asked that they sell him the rest of the coins, though he wouldn't be able to cash them out right that second. As Sarah had no desire to tote a bunch of silver coins around, she agreed to his deal. The dealer supplied a canvas tote for the money and even threw in a black Stetson that Nate had been eyeing. As Nate was mostly dressed in Sarah's father's clothes from the waist up, the hat went a long way toward making him feel a little more like the man he usually was.

"Did this guy say how you're supposed to go about the exchange?" Nate asked as they drove away.

"Yeah. I'm to go to room eight and knock three times."

"He's going to be there?"

"I guess so. He isn't exactly forthcoming."

"She's just quietly sitting in a motel room? That doesn't sound very plausible."

"You have to remember that they're threatening her with my safety. She acts up, they take it out on me."

Nate narrowed his eyes but kept his gaze straight ahead. He didn't know Sarah's mother, but from what Sarah had said about her, he had doubts she was able to think much further ahead than her own welfare. He'd have to trust Sarah's faith in the woman, but it went against all common sense to meet someone like this on their terms.

Options? He couldn't think of any. Not only was he currently not in law enforcement, but even if he was, he would be powerless to act in a different state. Putting aside the ethics of paying off a goon, you had to remember it was only money—and Sarah's money, at that—and perhaps down the line, justice would be served.

He would play his part just as he'd promised. What else could he do?

SARAH STRAINED AGAINST her shoulder seat belt as though willing the truck to move faster. Reno traffic was unexpectedly heavy, but it petered out as they headed south. It took half an hour to get to Carson City and then they had to stop at a service station to ask directions to the Silver Dollar Motel.

The motel itself turned out to be in an almost deserted industrial area of town, bracketed by an old warehouse with its windows shot out and a fenced yard full of old vehicles.

The motel itself might have been cute at one time in its dim past. Now it was surrounded by weeds and didn't even appear to be in business. The sign out front included a huge neon figure of a cowboy lounging with his back against the marquee, his arms folded across his chest, his face set in a permanent smirk. Most of the bulbs surrounding his figure were broken. A smaller sign announced there were no vacancies. The parking lot was covered with dust and the chill February wind blew a few tumbleweeds along the snow-dusted pavement. The one visible car was pulled up in front of unit eight.

"Except for that car, this place looks like a ghost town," Nate said.

Sarah nodded, her mouth too dry to actually make words. How was this all going to go down? As they rolled across the parking lot, she saw Nate reach under his seat. When he caught her watching him, he admitted he didn't want to take his wallet into this situation and she was glad he'd thought to leave it behind.

As Nate locked the rental truck, Sarah slowly approached the door of room number eight, her skin prickling with the sensation of being watched, the duffel bag heavy in her hand. She knocked the prescribed three times as Nate joined her on the step.

A big brute of a man with two silver eyeteeth opened the door. Bellows looked much the same as he had at the airport the only other time she'd seen him. A smaller man with thick curly gray hair and dressed in a golf shirt stood to the side. With a grunt from Bellows, the smaller guy patted Sarah and Nate down. All they found were Nate's truck keys, which he snapped back.

"Where's my mother?" Sarah said after a quick glance around the room, which seemed predominantly green from the carpet to the bedspread to the wall paint and was achingly absent of another person.

"Where's my money?" Bellows said, then, staring Nate in the eye, added, "And who the hell are you?"

Nate crossed his arms, and for a second, he looked like the human version of the cowboy out front. "My name is

Nate," he said in a Western accent new to Sarah. "I'm a friend of the family. Can't expect her to run around on her own, now can you?"

Bellows grunted and turned his back on Nate to address Sarah. "Your mom is close by. We got tired of her caterwauling. This place is empty, so she can yell all she wants as long as we don't have to listen to it. Two days was enough. Woman's got quite a mouth on her. Now, hand over the money."

"I want to see her first," Sarah said.

"You'll see her when I say you see her."

"No dice," Sarah said. "How do I know you'll keep your part of the deal?"

"Here's a—what do you call it?—a gesture of goodwill," the big man said and handed Sarah her handbag. She opened it to see her belongings as she'd left them: the phone in a side pocket, her house keys and hairbrush, her wallet with a few green bills showing. Was she supposed to be impressed by his honesty?

She shouldered her bag. "Let me see my mother, then you can see the cash."

The big guy looked at Nate. "Are you as stupid as she is? Has it completely slipped your mind who has a gun and who doesn't? Show them your gun, Benny, and don't be shy about using it if either one of them forgets the facts of life again."

Benny pulled out a lethal-looking gun and then tucked it back in his waistband.

"Just tell me where she is," Sarah pleaded.

"She's here in the motel. Now open that bag."

Sarah zipped open the bag and the two thugs fell on it like pirates on a keg of rum.

"Where is Diana Donovan?" Nate asked.

"Room twelve," Benny said. He was stacking up hundred-dollar bills like an accountant.

Nate reached for the door, but Bellows threw out an arm to stop him. "Not so fast, slick. The girl can go get her mother. You're staying where I can keep my eye on you."

"Is the door of her room locked?" Sarah asked.

"No."

Sarah left the room after exchanging meaningful glances with Nate. She hurried along the cold sidewalk to unit twelve and threw open the door.

Her mother lay straddled on the bed with hands and feet each tied to a bedpost. The gag in her mouth looked torturous, and her eyes, as they landed on Sarah, went from terrified to relieved in a blink. She pulled against the knots to the point that Sarah's fingers hurt trying to untie them.

"Calm down," Sarah kept saying. "You're safe now. Just relax so we can get you out of here." As she struggled with the knots on her mom's right hand, she saw the busted, bruised and swollen fingers and couldn't imagine how much they hurt, though her mother seemed oblivious to the pain.

Eventually Sarah managed to free all the knots and helped her mother sit on the side of the bed. Her jeans and pink T-shirt were studded with rhinestones that looked glaringly out of place in the shabbiness of the room.

For some reason, Sarah had left removing the gag for last, and as that came off, Diana Donovan licked her lips and rubbed her face with a jittery hand.

"Are you all right?" Sarah asked.

"I could have died!" Rivers of mascara had run down her face until her eyes looked like dark smudges. This impression was enhanced by the shiner, which Bellows had probably given her and which was now turning her left cheekbone shades of blue and purple.

Sarah tried to hug her, but her mother stood abruptly. "Did he give it to you?" she hissed.

"Sort of," Sarah said, knowing the *he* her mother referred to was her father.

"What do you mean, 'sort of'? Where is it?"

"I handed it over to the men in room eight," Sarah said, furrowing her brow. What else would she have done?

"All of it?"

"Of course."

"We could have bargained them down," her mother said.

Sarah felt sure her jaw dropped open. "Bargained with them? Look at you. They've…they've beaten you up and your fingers are broken and untreated."

"Right. And how will I afford to fix them now when you gave away all my money? What will I use to get back on my feet?"

"It's Dad's money," Sarah said softly, glancing away from her mother's swollen face. "And if you're talking start-up money for more gambling—"

"Of course I'm talking seed money, but it all belongs to snaggletooth now!" Her mother turned abruptly, staggered as though weak or dizzy, but she caught herself and left the room. By the time Sarah gathered her wits and followed, her mother was opening the door to room eight and disappearing inside.

STARTLED, NATE WATCHED Diana Donovan storm into room number eight, take a good look around and march on over to Bellows and Benny, who were still counting out their money around a tiny, scarred table. She stood over them and started poking and grabbing, swearing like a sailor and acting about as scared as a bulldog confronting a mouse.

This was Sarah's mother? She was a good six inches shorter, rounder, softer-looking with very pink skin stretched tight over her cheekbones, as though she was no stranger to plastic surgery. Even taking into consideration the woman's running makeup, bleached hair and the black eye, the differences were so striking they seemed impossible to reconcile.

A second later, Sarah erupted through the door, as beautiful as ever, but somehow changed. She lunged for her mother, who shook her off as she grabbed a fistful of dollars. The bigger of the two thugs grabbed Diana's right hand to make her release the dough, and that must have compressed her horribly mangled fingers. The scream that leaped from her throat could curdle milk. The big man slugged her, but it was like fuel to the older woman's rage. She yelled louder.

Nate couldn't just stand there. Using reflexes honed by years of hands-on experience at keeping the peace, he jumped into the fray and wrangled both men to the ground, delivering and receiving a fair number of punches in the process. Fists flew; screams flew; cash flew. He subdued the smaller of the men and was in the process of getting to his feet when the larger man grabbed him from behind with a stranglehold around his throat. He heard a deep thud, and the pressure lessened as the man's hands slid away. With a thump, the guy ended up facedown on the floor.

Nate looked up to find Sarah standing there with a metal waste can in her hands.

"Did you—"

"—whack him over the head?" she said. "I sure did."

Nate brushed his hair from his face and scooped his hat off the floor where it had fallen. His shoulder throbbed again, but that discomfort was mitigated by the sight of Sarah's smile as she surveyed the results of her handiwork. "Thanks," he said.

"Anytime."

Benny's eyes seemed to spin in opposite directions as he came around, while Bellows held his head and groaned. Nate relieved Benny of his gun and patted down the other one for a weapon. "He's clean," he said.

Diana started to scoop up more of the money, but Nate caught her hand. "What the hell do you think you're doing?"

"Taking what should be mine," she said. "There's enough here for a fresh start."

"They'll come after you," Sarah said as she set aside the trash can.

Diana kept cramming money in her pockets. "I'll go far away."

Nate shook his head. "You do that and they'll go after your daughter. Sarah will continue to be in danger."

"No, they won't. She'll be fine."

Nate pointed Benny's gun at her. "Put every penny back on that table."

She looked at him as though he was nuts. "Who the hell died and made you boss?" she demanded.

"Do it," Sarah said. She glanced up at Nate and added, "He's already killed one person today. I wouldn't push your luck."

Diana looked from one of them to the other, shoved her tangled, bleached hair away from her round face and sighed. She dug the money out of her pocket and threw it at the two men on the floor.

"Ladies? Time to go," Nate said, still holding the gun. Benny and Bellows were beginning to sit up and take notice of their surroundings.

He hurried both women to his truck, which had a double cab. He expected Sarah to slide in back with Diana, but instead she got into the front. Nate glanced at her face as he closed her door, taking in her huge blue eyes and mussed hair, her sweet lips and long throat, all absorbed into his brain and recorded for future reference in the time it took to blink. It felt like the end of the road for them—he had things he had to do, and from what he'd seen in that motel room, Sarah's hands were going to be full for a long time.

As he walked around behind the truck, he fought off a wave of melancholy. He wasn't ready to say goodbye to Sarah Donovan but he should have seen it coming.

Shots came out of nowhere, or so it seemed in the instant it took Nate to dive to the pavement. He still carried Benny's gun. Another shot alerted him to the direction from which the gunfire originated and he got off a round of his own before leaping to his feet. Someone was shooting from the abandoned building next door.

Sarah pushed open his door, then hunkered down low as he climbed inside. He jammed the key in the ignition and shifted into Reverse, sitting up fully as he steered away from the building and the shooter. His last sight was of Bellows and Benny standing at the motel door.

They looked as confused as Nate felt and he had the profound feeling they had nothing to do with the ambush.

So now who was gunning for him?

Chapter Eleven

"They're still shooting!" Diana Donovan screamed, and sure enough, Nate heard a bullet hit the rear of the truck. He glanced back to see the gunman had come out of hiding and was now standing out in the open wielding what appeared to be a rifle. Nate could make out nothing of the man's features and another bullet hitting the back window took care of him trying to.

"Get your head down," Nate shouted. "You, too, Sarah."

Both women ducked as yet another bullet hit what sounded like the bumper. Undoubtedly, the gunman was aiming for the tires. Another shot was followed by the tinkle of breaking glass and a scream from Diana. A quick glance at the rearview mirror revealed part of the sliding back window was now gone.

If Nate hadn't had passengers, he might have doubled back and headed right for the jerk. Instead he took a hard turn to the right. The small truck skidded a bit but kept to the road, and Nate immediately took a left turn and, at the next corner, another sharp right. There was no sign of pursuit, but he kept up the evasive maneuvers until they cleared Carson City and hit the road back to Reno.

"I think it's safe to sit up," Nate said, glancing at Sarah, whose expression looked terrified, all in all a logical reaction to the past few minutes.

"No, thanks," Diana Donovan called from the backseat. "I'm staying down."

Sarah, however, did sit up and twisted around in her seat. "Are you okay?" she asked her mother.

"No, I'm not okay. I'm covered with glass. What the hell is going on?"

"Good question," Sarah muttered as she turned her attention to Nate. "Did you notice the shots didn't start until you were walking around out there alone?" she asked.

Nate nodded. He'd noticed. It was pretty clear whom the intended target had been.

"Better head to the emergency room," she added with a nod toward the backseat.

"What's the point?" Diana grumbled. "I can't pay for anything."

"I'll cover it," Sarah said.

Diana sat forward, resting her hands on the back of Sarah's seat. "Did your father give you more money?"

"Yes," Sarah said.

"How much more?"

"Everything."

Nate kind of wished she hadn't said anything to her mother about the money, but talk about something not being his business.

"Is there a lot?" Diana asked, her voice anxious.

Sarah turned to face her mother. "Don't you want to know why he gave me everything?"

"Not particularly. Not after he turned his back on me."

"It's because he's dead, Mom. Murdered. I thought maybe you told the killers that I'd gone to Dad's house to get the money to rescue you, but now I'm beginning to think that's not the case."

"Of course I didn't tell anyone where you were going," Diana said. "How did Mike die?"

"He was shot."

"By this man you've taken up with?"

Nate cast his gaze into the rearview mirror, but he couldn't see the older woman.

"No."

"Are you sure?"

"Positive."

"So, how many of the coins do you still have?"

"Enough, but that's not how I'll cover your expenses. I have a little of my own money left after buying the plane ticket to come here. What I have is yours so you can get back on your feet. I'm hoping you'll give that gambling-addiction program another chance to help you."

"I'm not addicted!" Diana insisted. "I just like to have a good time."

"Think about the past few days," Sarah said, her voice soft and in vibrant contrast to her mother's nasal whine. "Do you really think the people who gamble for fun end up dealing with loan sharks and thugs, getting beaten up and held against their will?"

"I'm not other people," Diana said. "Things got a little crazy this time, but with your father's money…"

"No, Mom. You're not going to burn up Dad's money."

"What are you going to do with it?" she demanded.

"I don't know, but I'm not going to hand it over to criminals. You need help. I'm begging you to get it."

"I'll think about it," Diana said, and Nate could tell from her tone of voice that she was placating Sarah. It was probably part of her pattern, a little olive branch of hope extended with no heart behind the words, intended to end an unwinnable conversation without making a commitment.

But Sarah seemed content with the response. "Good. That's a start."

"As soon as I get my hand fixed up properly, I'm going to need my car," Diana added. "Where is it?"

"It's in Dad's barn. You'll have to wait until the police release it."

"Why would the police care about my car?"

"Dad was killed at his house, Mom. There were also other troubles. You don't need to hear about them right now, but I imagine the whole ranch will be a crime scene. Don't worry. I'll help you figure something out."

"I'm sorry I was so short with you earlier," Diana said, her voice suddenly softer. "No matter, we'll have lots of time to talk and get to know each other again. Days and days. Months. Years."

"Well, a little while, anyway. I do have a life I have to return to," Sarah said.

"Where?"

"In Virginia. I work for a great veterinarian there. I told you about it. I love working with the animals."

"Oh. Well, what's more important, people or critters? Besides, thanks to your father, you won't need to work anymore. You can move out here and be closer to me. Won't that be fun? I can show you around. Reno is a great town after dark."

Nate kept his thoughts to himself, but even without looking at Sarah, he could sense the deep sinking of her spirits. Was she wondering if she would ever be free of this woman's emotional grip? There was no way on earth he could help her, and so he concentrated on driving and thought nice thoughts about his own parents, bless their independent souls.

Diana gave him instructions, and within a few minutes, he pulled up next to the emergency-room entrance. Without a word to Nate, the older woman was out of the car in a flash, pausing by Sarah's door. Cubes of safety glass glittered on her shoulders and from her hair.

Sarah glanced at Nate, then opened her door and turned her attention to her mother. "Go get out of the cold, Mom. I'll be with you in a minute."

As Diana walked inside the building, Sarah turned back to face Nate. "Aren't you coming in to have your arm looked at?"

"I'll wait until I get to Shatterhorn," he said. "I don't want to answer questions about a gunshot wound more than once. You should take your father's notebook." He opened the console compartment between them, but she closed it before he could withdraw the battered notebook.

"No, you keep it."

He nodded.

"I'm sorry about my mother," she added.

"You have nothing to be sorry about."

"Yes, I do. She's a little on the self-centered side. She's used to having somebody look after her. After Dad there was a string of guys. She must be between men now. That may have been what triggered the latest gambling episode. I don't know…."

"It's okay," he said. "She's your mother."

Sarah nodded, but still she lingered until at last she reached across the console and touched his arm. He put his hand over hers and leaned toward her. Their kiss was short and circumspect, but as always, there was the pulsating awareness of her that burned beneath Nate's skin.

"I'm scared about you going off alone after what just happened in the parking lot," she said softly, her lips moving against his. "And then there was that guy this morning…. Can you believe that was only a few hours ago?"

"I've known you a little less than twenty-four hours," Nate said, running his fingers along her curved jaw.

"But they've been a very intense twenty-four hours," Sarah said. She closed her eyes and leaned her face against his palm. He could feel a wisp of dampness, as though a stray tear had hidden in her lashes. "I don't want to let you go."

"Come with me," he said, brushing his lips along her temple.

"I can't."

"You're going to have to explain your part in all this sooner or later, you know."

"I know." She pulled away a little and squared her shoulders. "You saw my mother. I have to stay with her at least through tomorrow, help her get settled, then I'll rent a car or something and drive up to Shatterhorn. Will you still be there?"

"That depends," Nate said, not going into detail. It depended on whether he survived the rest of the day, whether he was charged with murder or whether he was free to go back to Arizona, which was the option his gut told him to take if possible. Sarah was buried in issues with her family and he was still half-dead inside and on the heels of a breakup. Twenty-four hours of living on the edge with Sarah had meant a lot to him. She meant a lot to him, but she was unavailable, and perhaps he was, too.

Maybe that was just the story of his life.

"I programmed my cell-phone number into your phone while we drove," she said. "Call me."

"Sure," he said, knowing he wouldn't put himself through any more goodbyes.

"I had such big plans for us, you know, for tonight. I guess I wasn't thinking clearly about reality," she said.

"That happens under duress," he said. "Don't worry about it."

"But—"

He cupped the back of her head and kissed her again, putting an end to words that didn't mean as much as the touch of her lips. This time he didn't care who saw or even if the gunman lurked nearby. Her lips tasted just as good as they had the night before; his longing for her hadn't diminished. She would now join his personal string of opportunities lost and regrets to ponder.

When they came up for air, he released his grip on her. "Your mom is waiting for you," he said. "Take care, Sarah."

"You, too," she whispered as she slipped out of his truck and out of his life.

SHERIFF ALAN GALLANT greeted Nate with a hearty handshake. "It's been a while since we saw you," Gallant said, peering into Nate's eyes. "After what happened the last time you were here, I guess you haven't felt much like visiting us. How's your pal Detective Foster?"

"Alex is fine," Nate said. "He would have been here with me, but he couldn't land because of the weather. I'm not here for a visit, though. I have a story I have to tell you and I'm afraid it includes a couple of dead men."

"Cripes," Gallant said with a grimace as he forced his ample frame into a protesting wooden chair. He looked over his shoulder and said, "Larry, bring coffee. Patty, you better get this on tape." After the coffee was delivered and the equipment switched on, Gallant looked straight into Nate's eyes. "What's going on?"

"I'm not sure," Nate said. "First I should ask you if anyone called in a fire at the Donovan horse ranch or reported a body."

"What? Hell no. You mean Mike Donovan? What did he do now?"

"Nothing that I know of. He's dead, Sheriff."

"He finally pissed someone off bad enough to get himself killed?" Gallant immediately shook his head and looked contrite. "Sorry, I know he was a friend of yours. That wasn't a nice thing for me to say. Tell me what you know."

Nate launched into an account of what turned out to be a multilayered story. It took him an hour to tell it, and by that time, Nate had handed over the film he'd used to record the original condition of Mike's body, crime-scene units had been sent out to both the river cabin and the ranch house and investigations had been launched. Once they were alone, Gallant swiveled to face Nate and lowered his voice. "Tell me again about Peter Jacks."

Nate once again repeated the morning's events. He downplayed Sarah's role, but there was no way to leave her out of everything, as her fingerprints would be all over the cabin and the abandoned snowmobile, so he also explained about her family trouble and how she would be here the day after tomorrow to clear up her part in the proceedings. As promised, he left out any mention of the coins.

And that made explaining the origins of Benny's gun, which he handed over at once, a little tricky. He couldn't keep the weapon nor did he want to—who knew what crimes it had been used to commit—so in the end he gave a good description of Benny and Bellows and told a watered-down version of the situation in Carson City. Finally, he kind of threw up his hands. "Sarah will clear it up when she gets here."

This lame statement caused the sheriff's thick brows to furl, but he bagged the gun and let it go—for now.

Nate also admitted that yet someone else had taken shots at him. He really had no choice in the matter as the rental company was sure to notice all the damage and report it. The sheriff asked if he wanted protection and he waved the offer away. Protection from whom? Unfortunately, he could provide precious few facts and Gallant informed him he would take care of alerting Carson City police. He seemed to be under the impression the shooting was related to the ransom and Nate let that assumption stand.

"Which brings us back to Peter Jacks," the sheriff said with a shake of his big head. "I knew the boy was having trouble. Him and Stew's boy both."

"You mean Stewart Netters, the editor of the paper? So we're talking about Jason?"

"Yeah. The kid hasn't been right since the shooting. Having both those girls gunned down right in front of him, to say nothing of the other two dead kids— I don't know. Maybe it's survivor's guilt."

"Yeah," Nate muttered. He'd thought a lot about survivor's guilt. Unfortunately, he hadn't come up with a way to turn it off.

"Not that people haven't tried to help," Gallant continued. "There's a relatively new organization around, started by a man named Morris Denton. He calls it B-Strong. It concentrates on building character and self-esteem. Some of the local kids have attended summer programs and weekend workshops, things like that. The hope is positive reinforcement will empower them. It certainly seems to have empowered Thomas Jacks."

"Thomas had been part of this camp?"

"Yeah. Of course, after the shooting we interviewed anyone who had ever talked to the kid. No one up there had a thing to offer."

"Did you meet Denton?"

"Briefly. He was out of the country when the shooting occurred and was horrified by Thomas's actions, just like everyone else." He shook his head. "Lots of people rallied round Peter after the shooting, but there were some, too many, who seemed to be waiting around for him to do something terrible like his brother did. I've known the Jacks family for years. Peter and Thomas were on the same soccer teams as my own kids, went on the same campouts, attended the same church. When Thomas went berserk in the mall, the whole town suffered, but no one worse than his folks and his brother. There was no warning, no nothing."

"Is there anyone who thinks a foreign terrorist group might be involved?"

"Well, I think Netters did at first. He ran a couple of articles about something called People's Liberation, right after they took credit for the Hawaii shooting last December, but I think Thomas acted alone."

"Are you sure?"

"The sheriff's department found no link between him and any terrorist group. Neither did the city cops or the feds, at least as far as I know."

"How about the possibility Thomas was in league with another individual, you know, another kid, maybe?" Nate stopped short of naming Jason.

"Nope. It's pretty much like the mayor says. In recent years there has been a rash of domestic acts of violence across the country, where one citizen directs his rage at a random group of others."

"The mayor said that?"

"He's running for office. His bottom line is America for Americans, take care of yourself, do for government, don't wait around for government to do for you. His rhetoric might sit easier if he was a self-made man, but he's riding on family money. Still, what he says makes sense to lots of folks. I wouldn't bet money on the other guy winning."

"Do you think the mayor's sentiments made sense to Mike?" Nate asked.

"Up to a point. Mike took things a step further. He was convinced these random acts were related, that there was someone behind them. In my humble opinion, teenagers aren't generally disciplined enough to organize some clandestine movement."

Gallant paused to scratch his jaw. He wore horn-rimmed glasses, and those came off next for a quick inspection before once again returning to the perch on his nose. "Around here, gun permits doubled after the shooting," he said, his voice softer. "No one felt safe. And now this thing with Peter. It's going to absolutely kill his parents."

Nate's gaze drifted to the view out the window. There was still snow on the ground and the skies were a clear, cold gray. A winter world, to be sure, but was it really such a threatening place that people were afraid to go outside without a weapon in case their neighbor went nuts? Scary thought.

But look at Peter Jacks. What had gone wrong?

Peter, lying by the river with an ax in his back, thanks to Nate. "Did Mike try to help anyone?"

The sheriff sipped at his cold coffee before answering. "Mike was in here all the time, spouting his favorite conspiracy theory about some evil mastermind at work behind the scenes."

"Did he say who he suspected?"

"Not to me."

"Did he ever mention anything about the Washington Memorial or Monument?"

Gallant looked slightly pained. "Yeah. I heard about that."

"Did you tell anyone with the authority to guard, say, the Washington Monument on Presidents' Day?"

"Nate, now listen. The feds are always on the alert during crowd situations and especially on holidays. You think the little old sheriff from Shatterhorn, Nevada, is going to tell them something they don't know? For that matter, do you think they'd actually listen to me?"

Nate took a deep, frustrated breath. "I guess you have a point."

"Well, Mike sure as heck didn't think I had a point. I told him to leave the matter to the government and all those counterterrorist experts. If there was really some kind of conspiracy, domestic or foreign, they'd find it. But he wouldn't listen. If he wasn't lecturing me or the city council or trying to get things published in the paper, he was showing up at meetings where he didn't belong. Made a real nuisance of himself."

"Enough so that someone wanted to kill him?"

Gallant shook his head. "Heck, I don't know. Does his daughter have any idea who wanted her father dead?"

"No," Nate said and, anxious to change the subject away from Sarah, added, "I'd like to get my truck towed into town and repaired."

"You're kind of hard on your vehicles," Gallant said with a chuckle.

"Very funny. I'm not the one who keeps shooting at them."

The sheriff sobered right up. "I'll let you know as soon as you can. I need to go talk with the Jacks family and then drive out to the Donovan farm. You come back in the morning, okay? Don't leave town, by the way."

"Am I being charged with something?"

"Not right now. But you're in the business—you know there will be more questions."

"I've taken a leave of absence for a few months," Nate said.

Gallant looked surprised. "Mind if I ask why?"

"Just trying to get some things straight. I needed a little time."

"I see." He pried himself out of his chair and took his jacket from a hook on the wall. "If Sarah doesn't show up by tomorrow night, I'm going to get a warrant to bring her in for questioning."

"She'll be here," Nate said, not sure if she would or not. "All right if I go now?"

"Sure. Where are you staying?"

"I don't know."

"Try the Motorcoach Inn. It's a little on the old side, but they got cable TV, a free breakfast, and the coffee shop next door isn't bad for dinner."

Nate stood and offered a hand. The resulting shake just about jarred him out of his boots. He put his hat back on his head and buttoned up Mike's old coat, something else he would need to replace.

"How about your arm?" the sheriff asked, apparently noticing the gingerly way Nate pulled on the jacket. Nate had told him about the shot, of course, and the fact that he believed he'd wounded the shooter in return.

"I'll have it looked at tomorrow," Nate said. "All I want now is something to eat, a hot shower and eight uninterrupted hours in the sack."

He figured he'd be lucky to get even one of those.

NATE ASKED FOR a corner table away from any windows at the back of the restaurant and took the chair that faced the door. He'd come across the parking lot to eat as soon as he'd checked in, before taking a shower, even, and imagined he looked like something his dog had pulled from under a rock. He'd had a feeling, however, that once undressed and clean, he'd fall into a coma. It had been a good long time since he'd had anything to eat, and his stomach was grumbling.

Now he watched everyone who entered, looking for anyone who acted uncomfortable or out of place. A man would have to be nuts not to be cautious when two different people on two different occasions tried to kill him on the same day. And maybe yesterday, too... What had he done to deserve all this very unflattering—and deadly—attention? He had absolutely no idea.

Though he detested using a cell phone in a restaurant, there was no one else seated close by, so he employed the time between ordering and eating to make a call to Alex Foster's house. Hopefully he'd be home by now or Jessica would know where he was. But Nate's call went straight to voice mail. The message he left was short and to the point.

Dinner was hot, substantial and filled some of the hollow spots that had been growing inside him for the past couple of days. His waitress resembled Debbie, his ex, right down to her lush curves and black curls. She had the same high-pitched laugh, too, the same way of using a hundred words to say what could be accomplished with ten, and it came as something of a surprise to Nate that he was glad he wasn't going to spend his life dealing with Debbie's nonstop chatter.

Which brought to mind Sarah's way of talking, the words she chose, the sound of her voice, and from there, it didn't take too big a leap to zero in on the shape of her lips as she formed those words, the taste of her mouth and the stirring in his loins that thinking of all this created.

He needed some cold air on his face, and he paid his bill, leaving a big tip for his waitress in a vague, convoluted apology to all the ways he'd failed Debbie. Maybe she'd been right. Maybe she hadn't left him; maybe he'd left her.

Before Nate walked back into the night, he asked to

borrow the restaurant's phone book. He wasn't sure the motel room would have one, and he knew once he was close to a shower and bed, he wouldn't want to leave again. Using his own cell, he first dialed the airport, where he asked if Alex had landed his plane and was assured he hadn't. Then Nate called the mayor's house. A male employee with a crisp, cultivated voice answered and revealed the mayor was out of town until the day after tomorrow. Leaning against the wall, Nate flipped through Mike's notebook and decided to call the editor of the newspaper, Stewart Netters. Though it was late, the man answered the phone himself. He seemed pleased to hear from Nate and agreed to meet him in his office the next afternoon, even though it was a Sunday.

Nate had to find Mike's killer, not only to avenge his friend, but because there was the off chance that the attempts on his own life were somehow connected to Mike's murder. Nate wanted to figure this out, put a stop to it and get back to Arizona and his ranch and his life. He'd hoped to find answers of some sort in Shatterhorn, but what he had gotten were more questions.

It was dark by the time he walked outside, and the melting snow had started to refreeze, making it slippery as all get-out. He kept to the shadows, waiting for something to happen—a gunshot, a racing engine, heck, a bomb landing at his feet. He found himself looking over his shoulder, walking as fast as he dared. He hated feeling vulnerable, and it was a relief when he closed the door and locked it, sliding home the deadbolt, claiming his space.

"His space" was hopelessly old-fashioned, but what it lacked in character, it made up for in cleanliness. The drapes were closed, the bed looked comfortable and he'd hope for the best when it came to the shower behind the closed bathroom door.

He wasted no time easing his arm out of the sleeves of the jacket and shirt, both Mike's. On his way back to Shatterhorn, he'd stopped at a clothing store, where he'd bought himself some essentials. That bag sat on the chair beside the door, promising clean, warm clothes that actually fit for the next morning. He fought off a yawn as he stripped off the rest of his things.

He was putting his watch on the nightstand when he heard a shower go on so close by it had to be right next door. He groaned. If his neighbor was using this exact time to shower, what would that do to his own water pressure in a place this ancient?

Wait a second. Did he really care? No, not really. A hot trickle would do for tonight.

He opened the bathroom door to find that the water sounded as though it was running in his room because it was. Steam billowed out of the corner shower. Did the unit next door share this bathroom or had the motel mistakenly double-booked the room? He stared at the opaque shower door, trying to discern if the trespasser was male or female, but it was useless. He grabbed a towel from the rack and tied it around his waist as he considered the best way to handle the situation.

And that was when the clothes hanging on a hook behind the door caught his attention. He didn't recognize the white dress, but the equestrian boots sitting in a corner—they were a different matter. He blinked a couple of times and really opened his weary eyes. A purse the color of an old saddle perched on the back of the vanity and beside it sat a brand-new box of condoms. A smile spread his lips. He was suddenly wide-awake.

Chapter Twelve

Sarah jumped as the shower door opened. Even though she knew whom to expect, the past couple of days had cautioned her to be prepared for surprises, but this time there was no gunman, no threat, just Nate standing there giving her a lingering once-over, wearing nothing but a white towel.

And from the look in his eyes, to say nothing of the obvious engorgement beneath the terry cloth, he was just as happy to see her as she was to see him. She hadn't been sure he'd feel that way. Every inch of her body burst into excited flames that made the steamy water feel tepid against her heated skin.

"Are you going to stand there all night and ogle me?" she said.

"Not *all* night. Mind if I join you?"

She smiled. "What do you think?"

"I think I've never seen anyone in the world look better wet and naked." He threw aside the towel as he stepped into the small shower and closed the door. He slipped his arms around her waist. "How in the world did you find me?" he asked.

"I looked in every motel parking lot until I found a truck covered with bullet holes with a cardboard insert in the back window. Then I told the guy in the office I was your wife."

"So much for security."

"Has anyone else tried to…well…"

"Kill me? Not since Reno. And now you're here. The sheriff will be beside himself."

"And how about you?" she asked, staring into his eyes. "Are you beside yourself, too?"

"I'm giddy," he said and nuzzled her neck. She knew how he felt about seeing her, at least in a physical way. There was no hiding that.

"I brought you a present," she added.

He opened his hand and she found that he'd opened the box of condoms and brought one with him into the shower. She threw back her head and laughed. He put an end to that by pulling her against his powerful chest and claiming her lips.

The kiss started out hot and quickly boiled over. Sarah had never quite been kissed that way before, even by Johnny. So deep and long, like intercourse with tongues. Maybe it was because she'd brazenly initiated this scenario with Nate or maybe it was because she hadn't been positive he would welcome her, but she felt dizzy with the desire to touch and explore every solid, throbbing inch of him as his fingers set off discovering her.

He backed her against the tile and leaned in to kiss her neck, licking her ear, his hands gently fondling her breasts, his mouth dipping to suck rock-hard nipples, his erection hard against her abdomen. "I want to take it slow," he said, his voice almost a whisper, but that just fanned the fire, and she knew if this wasn't consummated within seconds, she would come completely undone. Kiss led to kiss, water sprayed and dripped. He touched her between her legs, his fingers gentle but insistent, his need echoing her own. She closed her eyes, consumed with passion, desperate to be closer. He lifted her bottom in his hands and she wrapped her legs around him; somehow he'd managed to put on the condom while she'd been soaring who knew where, and then he was inside her.

She gasped with the pure vibrancy and strength of his thrusts, the way he filled every crevice of her body from her brain to her toes, like an invading army with a take-no-prisoners approach. Her eyelashes fluttered against her cheeks and she saw his face through the water, both confident and lost, suffused with ecstasy that drove her over the edge at the same moment he leaned his head against her throat and exploded inside of her.

For several minutes, he kissed her, still holding her against him, then her feet touched the tile and she opened her eyes.

The smile on his face as he looked down at her was one of wonder. He smoothed her hair away from her face. "You're the sexiest, warmest, most slippery lover in the world," he whispered, his eyes devouring her. "So much for making it last," he added.

She touched the skin around the wound on his shoulder, but he didn't flinch. "You can make it last next time," she said. "Let me wash this wound for you."

He leaned against the shower wall as she found the tiny bar of soap and worked it into a lather against the hair on his chest, gently rubbing the resulting suds against his wounded skin. It really did look 100 percent better, and from the way he'd made love to her, she knew it must feel better, as well. From his biceps to his well-defined pectorals, down lower to his washboard abs, she followed the newly cleaned and rinsed skin with small kisses, smiling when he groaned with pleasure.

This time, they ended up in the bed, still damp but oblivious to anyone or anything but each other. And this time he made it last so long that the sheets all but incinerated.

When at last they were both replete, they lay in the dark, wrapped in each other's arms, tucked beneath the quilt and blankets, warm and content. Sarah had been exhausted when she got off the bus from Reno, but now she felt all tingly and strangely ravenous.

"I didn't expect you here tonight," he whispered against her hair.

"I like to be unexpected."

He kissed her forehead. "Come on, Sarah, tell me."

"Tell you what?"

"Where's Diana? The last I heard, you felt you had to stay in Reno a day or two to help her get settled."

Sarah cuddled deeper in the crook of his arm. "Nate, come on, I don't want to talk about my mother right now, okay?"

The bed shifted as he transferred weight to his side to reach the bedside lamp. Sarah blinked against the light, and when she looked at him again, she found his gray gaze focused on her face.

"Oh, all right," she said, partially sitting up but keeping the blankets close for warmth. "She refused to stay at the hospital and they said it wasn't necessary anyway. She wanted to go back to her apartment, so I took her there." Sarah rested her head atop her bent knees. All the peace she'd discovered in this room with this man seemed to be fizzing away like fragile bubbles escaping a glass of champagne.

"What happened?" he asked, sitting beside her now. He kissed her shoulder, and when she turned her head to look at him, his lips moved to her mouth.

"I took a shower and borrowed some clothes from her. She asked me to go down the block to the store to get something we could fix for dinner, so I did. When I got to the counter, I found I didn't have any cash."

"Had Bellows robbed you?"

She shook her head. "I know there was money in my bag when he gave me back my stuff. I saw it. But at the store, I literally didn't even have a single dollar. I'd paid for Mom's care at the hospital with a credit card. There was only one person who had been alone with my wallet since then, and you can guess who that was."

"How much did she take?"

"A hundred dollars or so. I put the groceries on a debit card and went back to her place, but I was on foot, so this all took a while. She was gone when I got there. No note, no nothing. I wondered if those two men had come after her again, or maybe Poulter had heard she suddenly had money.... I don't know. I was just about to call the police."

"Why didn't you?"

"Because one of her neighbors knocked on the door and asked if she was back yet. He wanted the twenty bucks she owed him. I assumed he'd been aware she was missing for a few days and started to explain, but he stopped me. He'd met up with her while walking down the sidewalk an hour or so before and had asked her for his money. She'd told him she was just going to go get it. She'd be back soon."

"Uh-oh."

"Yeah. I obviously went down the same sidewalk. The first place I came to was a hole-in-the-wall bar, and sure enough, there she was, black eye, bandages and all, playing the slots, drinking whiskey and flirting with someone I imagine she saw as a good prospect. Don't ask me what the guy was a good prospect for because I'm not going to tell you."

"What did she say when you spoke to her?"

"Who says I spoke to her?"

"You didn't?"

"Nope. I walked back to her place and left her a note telling her I was going to Shatterhorn to settle things with the police and would bring her car back in a few days. I'm not even sure why I did that much." She sighed deeply.

"But, Sarah, this is a pattern with her and her addiction, isn't it? Why did you choose this time to walk away?"

She looked straight into his eyes. "Because of you."

"Me?"

"Yeah. I could tell you were disappointed when I didn't agree to come back here with you. I could also tell that you were about to walk away from whatever is happening between us."

He didn't respond, so she continued. "When I saw her sitting in that bar and going at the slot machine, it all just gelled in my head. Someone is trying to kill you, and there I was, wasting my time with someone who didn't need me, not really. You've done nothing but protect me from practically the moment we met. With you, I can make a difference. I can watch your back. My presence will mean something. With her, I'm just an obstacle on the way to getting what she wants, and that's been true my whole life. So I chose to go where I could make a difference. I chose you."

He smiled at her, but was there also a flash of panic in those foggy gray eyes? Maybe she'd said too much. She smiled to lighten the mood. "Honestly, I'm just tired of being angry with her. She sneaks around, she connives and she lies. I'm done." Sarah chanced another glance at Nate. "Does that make me a horrible person?"

"I'm the wrong person to ask," Nate said.

"Why?"

He rested his forehead against her shoulder. "I've lied to you, too, Sarah."

"Oh, God, I don't want to hear this," she said. "Okay, what are you, still engaged? Oh, no, you're not already married, are you?"

"No, nothing like that. It's just that I'm not a cop anymore."

"That's it? Why?"

He swallowed and studied his hands. "Why am I not a cop or why did I keep it from you?"

"Both, I guess."

"I didn't want to say it out loud. I guess that's the answer to why I didn't tell you. As for the other, well, I took a leave to try to figure things out." He cast her a swift look and added, "The sheriff of our county is a real political type with eyes set on becoming governor. He wants hungry go-getters on his team. When I admitted that didn't really define me anymore, he encouraged me to run for sheriff when he left. I don't know if I want that. I don't know who I am anymore."

"I know who you are," she said, looking deep into his eyes as she ran her fingers along his jaw and up into his hair. Her last relationship had ended over a year before, and since then, she'd sworn off men, thinking they were all alike and you couldn't trust a single one of them.

She'd been wrong.

"You're kind and generous and sexy as all get-out. You're strong, Nate."

"Strong men don't run away," he mumbled.

"Do you call what you've been doing the past two days 'running away'? Really? Listen, I read something once that makes sense to me now that I've gotten to know you. It was about a study done with people who survive horrendous accidents or incidents. They found that the more a person was actually responsible for the safety of others or perceived themselves to be, the harder recovery was for them. So a pilot or a stewardess suffered a heck of a lot more than a passenger. That's what you're fighting, the feeling that you should have been able to subdue Thomas Jacks, when the truth is you were as unarmed as everyone else at that mall."

"But—"

"No, Nate. No buts." She kissed his neck. "You know, actions speak louder than words. How about you come closer and I'll demonstrate what kind of man you are?"

She didn't have to ask twice.

THEY AWOKE EARLY the next morning, still tangled in each other's arms. Nate had wondered if Sarah would feel shy or awkward with him after the night they'd spent, but her eyes and lips were as warm as ever, and a dangerous warmth glowed in his heart.

"You didn't have a nightmare last night," she whispered against his neck. "Or did you?"

"No," he said. "I'm not sure if it's because I barely got any sleep or because you're here. Either way, you get the credit."

She kissed his nose. "I'll put it on your therapy bill."

He dressed in his new clothes while Sarah put on the white dress that must belong to her mother. It was a little short and loose, but she cinched it in at the waist with her own leather belt. Dressed in the white wool sheath with the boots covering her legs, she looked incredibly put together. Nate fought down the desire to strip her out of her clothes.

They were too hungry to settle for the frozen waffles, tiny boxes of cereal and basket of bananas the motel served as their free breakfast. Instead they walked across the parking lot to the diner where it appeared half the town ate. Nate scanned the parking lot as they crossed, uncertain how best to shield Sarah in such a wide-open spot. In

a way he wished she'd stayed in Reno, where she would
have been safe.

Oh, hell, who was he kidding?

They ordered pancakes, bacon, coffee and juice and sat
side by side at the only two open seats, which happened
to be at the counter. It was the first real meal they'd ever
eaten together.

Nate had given the place and its patrons a once-over
before they sat down. If it had been him looking for an opportunity to pick someone off, he would have staked out
this café the night before and would now be sitting behind
a newspaper, biding his time, waiting for the opportunity
to attack, which would present itself sooner or later.

He could see no one lurking suspiciously behind the
morning paper. It might have been a big relief if he had.

Sarah finally had the opportunity to study her father's
notebook as they ate, and she finished scanning the pages
as they drove to the sheriff's office. "It looks like one's
been torn out," she commented.

"I saw that."

"That might be important," she said.

"Or it might be part of his editing process. Maybe he
just didn't like what he'd written."

She closed the book and wrapped a rubber band around
the pages. "I can't believe the leaps he made. *Pearl* refers
to Pearl Harbor? And he connected a Fourth of July shooting with these other situations. But really, they happened
all over the country, didn't they?"

"Yeah. What they have in common is young shooters
who all either killed themselves or were killed, and holidays like the Fourth of July, Labor Day, Veterans Day,
the anniversary of the attack on Pearl Harbor," Nate said.

"And what national holiday is next? Presidents' Day?

That's, like, tomorrow, isn't it? I've sort of lost track of the date."

"Tomorrow," Nate repeated, a little stunned. He'd lost track, too.

"What about the twenty-eight circled in red?"

He shook his head. "Not sure. By the way, have you ever heard of a guy named Morris Denton?"

She seemed to consider his question for a second before responding. "Can't say I have. Should I know who he is?"

"Not necessarily. I've heard his name mentioned in connection with a support organization focused on youth."

"Dad didn't mention him, too?"

"Not in those pages, which seems odd."

"Maybe that's the page he ripped out."

"And maybe he just discounted the guy. Maybe, maybe."

"What about Washington and a memorial?"

Nate cast her a quick glance. "I'm wondering if he meant 'monument,' as in the Washington Monument."

"Oh, no. Nate, who do we warn? Maybe there'll be another shooting tomorrow. We've got to try and stop it."

"This is all suppositions and connecting dots that may or may not go together. Just because there've been several events on weakly linked days doesn't mean the explanation is a huge plot. What would be the point of such a thing? Anyway, your dad was trying to make this point, but no one was listening to him. No one took him seriously."

"Not even his own daughter," Sarah said with a shake of her head.

"If it helps anything, I didn't score high on the list, either."

"At least you came when he called."

"I didn't come for him. I told myself I did, but it's not the truth. Anyway, we have a full day ahead of us. First the sheriff and then the editor of the paper."

"You're going to ask Netters what he and my dad talked about?"

"Yeah."

"I wonder how Jason is doing. I heard he was at the mall that day and that a couple of his friends were shot—" She stopped abruptly.

Nate knew his whole body had tensed as she spoke.

Her hand floated over to touch his thigh. "Me and my big mouth," she whispered. "For a second I forgot you were there with them."

"I wish I could forget," he said, and they finished the drive in silence.

SHERIFF GALLANT GREETED them with the news that he'd released both cars, and as he spoke with Sarah privately, Nate arranged to have the vehicles towed from the ranch while one of his deputies went out to catalog the damage to the rental. He was lucky the garage was willing to tow on a Sunday—a lot of small-town businesses shut down completely on the weekends.

Nate joined Gallant and Sarah after an hour or so. He was relieved to discover Sarah had been totally honest about everything, including the coins. Her father's will lay on Gallant's desk and the sheriff informed them they would all drive out to the ranch to clear up a couple of issues.

"The tech guys were out there all night gathering evidence," he said. "Looks like your attacker was shooting a .22. As for the coins, I don't see that the coins your father left you had much to do with anything. Still, best we recover them and get them someplace safe until this is all figured out."

"How did Peter Jacks's mom and dad take the news?" Nate asked, but if there was a dumber question in the world, he didn't know what it was. How many times had he had to tell someone's parents they'd lost their child, and how did they always take it? The fact Peter had been killed while attacking people only made it harder to hear, let alone understand.

"Pretty bad. I had the doctor come out and give Betty Jacks a tranquilizer. Peter's dad is just sitting there like a zombie."

"I wish I hadn't had to kill him," Nate said.

Sarah touched his arm. "You had no choice unless it was to let me die, and then he would have come after you."

"Sarah's story confirms what you told us, so we're not bringing any charges against you, Nate. The team that went over the cabin crime scene found out where Peter had been waiting over in the rocks, probably a couple of hours or more. There were a half dozen cigarette butts and some binoculars. If he hadn't been downwind from you, you probably would have known he was there because of the smell of the smoke."

"I wonder why he didn't just burst into the cabin while we were sleeping," Sarah said.

"I think he was working up his courage," the sheriff said, "but he might have also worried Nate was armed and wanted you out in the open to use as leverage."

Nate thought about it a moment and realized he'd probably never know the truth. The only man who knew was dead.

Wait—was that so? If it was, who had shot at him a few hours later in Carson City?

"Funny that Peter Jacks wasn't carrying any identification on him," the sheriff added. "Same with his brother, you know."

"Yeah."

"His folks say he's been out of town, just got back the night before he was killed."

"Did the M.E. find any gunshot wounds on Peter's body?"

"No. If you wounded someone out at the ranch, it wasn't him."

"Did his parents say where he'd been?"

"No. They say he's been hanging around with the Netters boy, Jason. I'll talk to him later. Still, I don't get the timing and I don't get the vendetta against you. It doesn't make sense."

"Did you hear back from the cops in Carson City?" Nate asked.

"Yeah, but there wasn't much to tell. By the time they got there, rooms eight and twelve had been wiped clean of prints. It's not even clear who owns the property. The gunman wasn't still hanging around the parking lot next door—no one thought he would be. And there are no neighbors to speak of, so no witnesses." Gallant paused before adding, "The police would like to ask you a few questions. They asked me to tell you to come on back and help them clear this up."

"I'll settle with them later," Nate promised. He had no idea what he could tell them—he simply didn't know much.

Revisiting the ranch was a gloomy, depressing affair. As Sarah had reported, the scorched house still stood. Mike's body had been removed the night before by the sheriff's department, but his ghost hovered just the same, tangled in the crime-scene tape, mingled with ashes, blowing in the breeze. Sarah got more and more withdrawn as they retraced the movements of two days before. The signs of their struggles—the broken glass, discarded saddle rifle, bloody bandages, bare walls and turned-up carpets—all looked garish in the cool light of day.

She'd grown up here, and in the past two days, her dad had been gunned down in cold blood and her mother had imploded. When they entered Skipjack's empty stall, her gaze went to the corner under the feed rack. By the time it was necessary for Nate to leave in order to meet up with Stewart Netters, she'd walked outside and stood staring up at the sky.

"Do you want to come to the newspaper office with me?" he asked her.

"I don't think so," she said. "Sheriff Gallant says he'll help me get the rest of the coins into town. He'll keep them safe in a police vault until the bank opens tomorrow, then I'll transfer them until the will is probated and all this legal stuff is worked out. That means I need a lawyer, too. I wonder if everything will be open on Presidents' Day."

"I don't think the banks are open," Nate said.

"Then I'll wait around until the day after tomorrow."

"Which begs the question of what we're going to do about this perceived threat your dad danced around concerning Washington and Presidents' Day," Nate muttered, as though talking to himself. He came up with an answer. "I'll call Dan Perry. He works with me, well, worked with me when I worked. His brother is an FBI agent. Maybe Dan can get him on board. I don't know."

"It's better than nothing," Sarah said, but her face revealed she thought it had as much chance of making a difference as he did, and that wasn't much.

"I also want to grab my suitcase out of Mom's car and go to the vet to see about boarding Skipjack for a while longer," she added.

"What will you eventually do with him?" Nate asked.

"I guess I'll sell him. Breaks my heart, though."

"Sell him to me."

She finally looked at him. "You?"

"Sure. I've got room for another horse. I can hook up a trailer to the truck and haul him back to Arizona with me. Truth is, I've grown pretty fond of him."

"There's a trailer out behind the barn you can use," she said. "In fact, you can have it."

"Deal. And you can come visit him whenever you're down my way."

Sarah smiled, the first one Nate had seen since she'd stepped foot on the ranch. He cupped her chin with his fingers and kissed her.

"Watch your back," she whispered as his lips left hers. "Don't forget someone wants you dead."

Chapter Thirteen

The newspaper office consisted of a half dozen rooms all accessible through a lobby outfitted with a glass door. It was empty on a Sunday afternoon, but there was a note on the receptionist's desk addressed to Nate, telling him to come back to the editor's office. As Nate had visited the past September, he knew his way around.

He entered a large office with a black desk at one end and a gathering of soft chairs at the other. The walls were covered with plaques and framed photographs surrounding a cabinet that Nate recalled housed marksman trophies that Stew Netters had collected over the years.

Netters, a compact fifty-five-year-old with a prominent Adam's apple, sat behind the desk. He was wearing a gray sweater and jeans. He had hair like his son's, though the blond strands were sprinkled with gray. He was busily taking notes while the mayor, seated in front of the desk, spoke.

Mayor Bliss was older than Netters by a couple of years and appeared extremely fit, sporting an out-of-season tan that showcased the brightness of his teeth when he smiled. He looked prosperous and sure of himself, and Nate had read that he won every election by a landslide. According to Gallant, this November would bring the same results.

A small lapel pin shaped like a waving American flag festooned the lapel of a dark blue suit.

There were hearty handshakes all around before Nate sat in the chair Netters indicated. "I understood you were out of town," Nate said, addressing the mayor.

"Just got home this morning."

"George flies himself all over the state," Netters said. "He's got his fingers in a dozen enterprises."

"Family business," Mayor Bliss explained. "My grandfather started Bliss Chocolate fifty years ago. The old man would turn over in his grave if I let it flounder, and that takes a hands-on approach, despite my elected office."

Netters drummed his fingers on the desktop as though he'd heard this spiel before. "Did you fly up from Arizona?" he asked Nate.

"No, this time I drove. I came to see Mike Donovan."

"I just heard he was killed the day before yesterday," Netters said, sitting forward.

"Yes, I know."

Enlightenment dawned on Netters's smooth face. "Of course. Gallant wouldn't release any names, but the buzz around town is there was a standoff of some kind out there. Did you have anything to do with that?"

Nate shrugged.

"How about giving me the story?"

"When the sheriff says it's okay," Nate said.

The mayor shook his head. His buzz-cut hair and the tan made him look ex-military. His mouth was on the small side and his lips were currently pursed. "It's the people's right to know what mayhem is brewing in their own city," he said. "Especially after last Labor Day. People are nervous, and another killing is just going to make things worse."

"There'll be more gun permits issued, you wait and see," Netters said.

"Speaking of which, didn't you just buy Jason a gun?" Bliss asked.

"I did," the editor said, nodding. "Although I debated the purchase."

"Why?" the mayor asked.

"He's young," the editor said.

"You're never too young to protect yourself and your family in these troubled times," Bliss commented. "People tend to think the government is going to take care of them. How much did that belief help those poor children at the mall last year?"

"Yeah, well, that's what Morris Denton told the boy. Anyway, I'm hoping it will give him a leg up come fall."

Nate thought of that troubled kid with a weapon and inwardly cringed. He also decided to play dumb about Denton. "Morris Denton? Who's he?"

"A philanthropist," Netters said. "He started this whole grassroots camp located on several acres up in the mountains. B-Strong, it's called. He gets kids from all over. Jason went to one of his workshops not long ago. He really seemed to change after that."

"In what way?" Nate asked.

"More sure of himself. Knows what he wants now. He's going to join the military when he turns eighteen in October. Helped him find himself."

"Have you ever met Denton?" Nate asked.

Netters shook his head. "Not yet, but I will. I think it's high time someone interviews Denton and takes a look around B-Strong. Too little is known about it and about Denton himself, especially since Thomas Jacks spent a few weeks late last summer at his camp."

"As a matter of fact, I wanted to ask about Thomas's

brother, Peter," Nate said. "Did he attend the workshop with Jason?"

Netters nodded. "I think he's the reason Jason wanted to go. They've been hanging out together."

"It doesn't sound as though you know Peter Jacks is dead," Nate said, watching both men.

Netters sat forward. "Dead? When? How?"

"Yesterday," Nate said. "He was about to shoot someone else."

Netters looked truly shocked. "My God."

Bliss spoke up. "Who was he going to shoot?"

"Mike's daughter, Sarah Donovan."

"Sarah is back in Shatterhorn?"

"She's the one who found her father's body," Nate said.

Stew Netters ran a hand through his sandy hair as though giving himself a moment for all this to sink in. He stood abruptly and took a few steps toward the door. "That damn Gallant is keeping things from me. I've got to get some reporters in here."

"Did you hurt yourself?" Nate asked, his voice kind of quiet. Netters had a pronounced limp.

"Damn arthritis in my left knee. Doc wants to replace it—I don't know, guess I'm dragging my feet. Where does that secretary keep my phone book?"

Nate studied the man as he searched a nearby shelf, looking for any sign of equivocation. Was arthritis really why he limped or had he been wounded by a bullet from Mike's saddle rifle, a bullet Nate had fired? There was just no way to tell without saying a lot more than he had any intention of saying. Instead, he asked, "Before you get back to work, would you please take a few minutes to tell me what you and Mike talked about the last time you saw him?"

Netters seemed to look longingly at the door, but eventually he limped back behind his desk and sat. His turned-down mouth and wrinkled brow suggested he didn't much like recalling Mike's last visit. Before he could launch into his story, the mayor spoke up.

"Was that the day Mike burst in here?" he asked. "You remember, Stew. You and I were just chewing the fat when Donovan showed up."

"Yeah, I remember," Netters said. "How could I forget? It was last week sometime. He pushed his way past the receptionist and plowed through the door."

"Why was he so angry?" Nate asked.

"Because I wouldn't print his half-baked theories about some countrywide conspiracy."

"He talked to you about those?" Nate asked.

"He talked to everyone. Man couldn't get enough of hearing his own voice," Netters said. "He thought there was one person behind all of the shootings with some crazy agenda, but he had no facts, just a lot of jumping from one big idea to the next. I don't think his feet ever touched down."

"So, he wanted you to interview him and float his theories?"

"That's about it. When I refused, he started insinuating I was part of the conspiracy. He called my newspaper 'biased.' Those are fighting words to a newspaperman like me. He was steaming hot under the collar, calling me names and threatening me."

"Threatening you in what way?" Nate asked.

"I don't remember," the editor said, his gaze shifting to the floor.

The mayor jumped in. "He said if he could prove you were part of this so-called conspiracy, he'd see you hang."

Netters seemed to blanch. "Donovan kept waving an old leather book wrapped up with rubber bands in my face.

He swore he had proof. He was fishing—I don't think he knew a damn thing. I mean, does he think he's the only one who's been working on figuring all this out? I've got my suspicions about what's going on, too, but you don't find me attacking people. Man, the jerk was practically foaming at the mouth."

"He wasn't the only one," Mayor Bliss said softly.

Netters frowned. "Okay, I admit it. I got angry, too. Who did he think he was, coming in here and acting like he had a right to say any damn thing he liked? I punched him, okay, I did, but it was provoked, wasn't it, George?"

The mayor shrugged. "Violence rarely solves anything, Stew—you know that. And Mike Donovan along with Mr. Matthews here and Alex Foster did come to the town's aid last Labor Day and help prevent that tragedy from being any worse. You yourself called them 'heroes.' I hailed them as patriots.

"Mike said he was going to call you and Alex," he added. "He said he wanted to get your feedback. Did he have a chance to talk to you before he died?"

"No," Nate said.

"You shouldn't have come here," the editor mumbled. "It's like you're a catalyst or something."

Nate didn't respond to the comment.

"Anyway," the editor continued, "all our compliments must have gone to Donovan's head." He looked at Nate and added, "After all, you didn't go psycho."

"Everyone copes in their own way," Nate murmured. "By the way, does the number twenty-eight mean anything to either of you?"

The mayor scrunched his brow. "Twenty-eight what?"

"I don't know," Nate admitted.

"Like a date?" Netters asked.

Nate shook his head. "Just wondered," he said.

The editor studied his hands for a moment, then looked defiantly at Nate. "I guess I shouldn't have punched Mike. I didn't like what he was insinuating. Rumors get started, a man's career goes up in smoke. You have to be careful what you say about people. Truth is, he was lucky I wasn't packing a piece or I would have shot him then and there."

His words, spoken softly and in light of what had eventually happened to Mike, fell like an atom bomb. And then someone cleared his throat and all three men turned to find Netters's son, Jason, standing right inside the door.

"Jason?" Netters said. "What are you doing here?"

Jason looked from his father to the mayor to Nate. "Nothing," he mumbled.

At that moment, the desk phone rang. Netters grabbed it, listened without taking his eyes off his son, then glanced at Nate. "It's for you," he said.

AFTER THE COINS had been locked in the evidence room at the sheriff's office, Sarah walked out to the sidewalk and checked her watch. Nate would still be at the editor's office and Sarah wanted no part of that. She'd heard the rumors about her father's behavior and she couldn't stand the thought of facing Stewart Netters.

But since she had some time and the garage was just a couple of blocks over, she might as well go get her mother's car and, more important, retrieve her suitcase from the backseat so she could put on some warmer jeans. As she walked, her brain finally kicked into gear. Now was her chance to drive out to the storage garage and see if her old boxes were in unit 118. She walked faster.

The garage was shorthanded on a slow, cold February afternoon. The green toad looked more dejected than ever as the man on duty, who had just finished replacing Nate's tires, looked up from his work.

"Bud," Sarah said, recognizing an old high school friend. "I didn't know you worked here."

Bud hit the button to lower the truck from the lift. "Hey, Sarah, it's been years," he said, reaching out to shake her hand, seeing the grease smudged on his and smiling instead.

She grabbed his hand and pressed it.

"Hey, your dress," he said.

She laughed. "It's okay. Boy, it's good to see you."

"You, too." He took a surprisingly clean rag out of his pocket and handed it to her. "I've been working with Dad since the economy took a downturn and I lost my job at the market. This pays better anyway, and seeing as I've got three kids to support, every bit comes in handy."

Sarah looked up from wiping away the tiny bit of grease on her fingers. "Three kids? Did you marry Janet Hawser?"

"Right after high school."

"That's great. You guys were a cute couple."

"Thanks. Hey, I heard about Johnny. Sorry. And now your dad. I don't know what this town is coming to. Getting so you're afraid to walk outside."

"Don't talk like that, Bud. You're raising kids. You have to have faith."

He grinned. "And a concealed-weapon permit. Listen, do they know who—"

"No, I'm afraid not. Not yet, anyway." She gestured at the car. "I came by to see if I can take this old wreck off your hands."

"Didn't Gallant tell you?"

"Tell me what?"

"It won't start. That's why we had to tow it in the first place."

Sarah's brows wrinkled. "Why wouldn't it start?"

"Heck if I know. I think the starter is shot, but Dad will have to check to make sure, and he won't be in until day after tomorrow. Then he'll have to order the part, but it won't take long to get here. Less than a day, probably."

Sarah sighed. "Rats."

"You need to get somewhere?"

"Yeah, just a couple of miles from here on the other side of the tunnel.... Wait, is Nate's truck drivable?"

"I guess so. It doesn't have a passenger window, but I got new tires put on and I vacuumed up the glass and stuff. It'll be pretty cold and you won't be able to lock it, is all."

"Then I'll borrow that, okay?"

"Do you have a key?"

She sighed again as the memory of Nate holding his keys in front of the window and repocketing them later surfaced in her mind. "No, he has them."

"I found a spare in a magnetic box in the rear tire well. Here, I'll get it for you and drive the truck out of the garage, okay?"

A few moments later, Bud gave her a hand up into Nate's truck, which he'd left running. She headed down the highway while cold air blew in through the broken window, chilling her to the bone. She zipped her jacket up to her chin with one hand and wished she had gloves and a hat. The road led through a long curvy tunnel at one point and the air in there seemed to have welled up right from the coldest spot in the world.

When she arrived at U-Lock Garages, she thought she'd made the trip for nothing, as the gate was closed. But as she sat there wishing she could figure out what code to input into the security lock, a white van approached. Sarah moved Nate's truck out of the way. The newcomer put in their number and the gate slowly opened, a sign on the inside warning that only one car should enter at a time. She quickly got behind the van and trailed it inside the gate, hoping it didn't take a code to get back out.

The row of tapioca-colored garages with red roofs stretched on for what appeared to be miles, crisscrossed now and again by roads leading to other rows of the same thing. The place had a desolate appearance. The van made the first left. Sarah followed the original row until a sign directed her to turn right. The numbers 114 to 118 were printed on a door that sat in the middle of a block of buildings. She parked the truck and tried the knob, which wasn't locked. A weak light went on, revealing four more metal rolling doors, two on each side of a ten-foot hallway. One-eighteen was the last unit on the right. She propped open the outside door with a wedge of wood that looked as though that was its intended purpose.

She could hear the buzzing of the timer light and hurried down the hall as she felt around for the paper-wrapped key in the depths of her handbag, where she'd deposited it the day before. Emerging with just the key, she closed it in her hand as she spied a piece of pink paper taped to the door. She unfolded that to find an eviction notice dated several weeks before, warning that the lock would be changed and the contents of the unit confiscated if her dad didn't settle his bill by the previous Friday. That was the day he had been killed. She stuffed the paper in her purse.

The padlock opened easily and she rolled up the door to reveal a very cold, very dark space piled high with shadowy boxes and other paraphernalia that looked as though it hadn't been sorted or attended to in years.

An electric lantern hung beside the door, and she flipped the switch, rather surprised when the light flickered on. Illumination did not mitigate the mess, but she did find that the boxes had been labeled with a black marker. Most seemed to hold old tax records and business papers from a decade or more before; some seemed to be her mother's old clothes, left behind in the divorce, but eventually, in the nearest corner, she came across the boxes she remembered packing so long ago. They had her initials printed on them in her dad's writing.

For a second, she stood there and tried to feel his presence in the tiny room, but she couldn't. He had to have been the one to bring everything here. She found a solid box to sit on, knowing the white wool dress would need a trip to the cleaners after this, and opened the first of three boxes.

Stuffed animals, rolled posters, boxes full of cheap jewelry, a collection of old CDs. She moved the box aside and opened the next one.

Under a layer of folded sweaters from a lifetime ago, she found the letters Johnny had written her, all stacked together, tied with a blue ribbon. She knew the exact date of the one she wanted and riffled through them until she found it. She opened the letter and stared at the words, reliving for a second that May day when Johnny had slipped it into her hand.

Baby, it began, *don't cry. I promised you...*

The resounding slam of a closing metal door banged nearby and Sarah almost fell from her perch atop the box. Still holding the stack of letters, she peeked out into the hallway, which was now heavily shadowed as the hall light had gone off and the outside door was no longer open.

Had the wind blown it closed?

Sarah stuffed the dozen or so letters into her purse and walked toward the door. She was afraid to open it because it felt as if someone was out there, waiting for her to emerge. She switched on the overhead light again and went back to relock the garage, then worked up her courage, finally opening the outside door.

The truck sat just as she'd left it, looking more than ever like a casualty of war with its broken window and line of bullet holes running down the side. She couldn't see anyone else, but there was a feeling of being watched that raised goose bumps on her arms. She glanced toward the highway, but it appeared empty, too. The wind had come up and blew down the narrow storage-lot roads like the icy breath of a ghost.

Sarah's heartbeat thumped in her throat as she scurried around to climb inside the truck. She locked the doors despite the missing window. Gunning the engine, she made a quick U-turn and headed toward the gate.

It turned out she did need a code to exit. Opening her window, she tried her father's birth date on the number pad, then the ranch address and a half dozen other numbers until she actually ran up against a memory of coming here with her father when she was a little girl. He'd made a big deal out of revealing the code was Sarah's birthday. She'd assumed he'd changed it. She popped in the numbers and watched as the gate rolled back.

She glanced at her watch as she turned onto the highway and realized this had all taken longer than she'd thought. Nate was probably wondering where she'd taken his truck. She drove faster, switching on her lights when she got to the tunnel.

It was about twenty feet long and made a curve in the middle. Sarah had driven through it a thousand times in her life and she knew you had to slow down to make the turn. The exit was also on a curve and as a kid she'd been terrified the first time she sat behind the wheel, then exhilarated as her expertise increased and it became something of a challenge to accomplish the turns smoothly.

Today she barely thought about it at all until she was aware of lights suddenly popping up in her rearview mirror. They were right behind her as though they'd come out of nowhere, dropped from above or wrenched from the roadbed. Her instinct was to hit the brakes, but that would have created a collision, so she was forced to speed up instead. The lights moved out from behind her as if to pass, and she gripped the wheel tightly because the idiot was going to be in the wrong lane at a critical moment on the curve. If someone was coming the other way, it was going to be nasty....

The larger vehicle suddenly loomed beside her. The next thing she knew, it had rammed in her door, shoving Nate's truck against the rock sides of the tunnel. The sound of screeching metal filled the cab as pieces of the truck flew off and disappeared in a flurry of sparks.

She tried applying the brakes, but the other truck was still pressing her inward. And then with a roar, it took off and sped out of sight around the curve. Meanwhile, Nate's truck was still ground against the wall as though it couldn't break free. She was almost around the bend herself. The truck finally broke away and shot out of the tunnel, Sarah fighting for control as the next curve was immediately upon her. She almost made it, too, but at the last minute, one of Nate's tires climbed a boulder, rearing like a stallion before falling back to earth in a lopsided crash. Sarah took a breath, thinking the worst was over, but it wasn't. The truck found a passage through the boulders and took off down the slope of the ravine, gaining speed.

Her foot still on the brake, Sarah rode the truck through bushes, headed for trees, snow flying in the wake until it came to an abrupt halt. The deployed air bag pinned her back against the seat.

By then she couldn't feel a thing.

Chapter Fourteen

By the time Nate left the editor's office, the skies above were dark and foreboding. While inside the windowless room, he'd overheard rumors that another storm was in the offing. Now, walking into the cold wind, it wasn't hard to believe.

He'd been called in by Gallant because Morris Denton had made an appointment to talk to the sheriff's department and Gallant thought Nate might want to sit in on the interview. While it had been hard to leave the editor's office at that exact moment, Nate had come, curiosity about Denton overcoming curiosity about how Stew Netters would get his giant foot out of his mouth and save face with his son.

"Now, what can we do for you, Mr. Denton?" the sheriff asked.

Denton was thin to the point of bony, with hands that seemed too large for the rest of his body. Dressed in jeans and a black sweater, he looked to be about forty, give or take a few years. Most disconcerting to Nate was the vague look in the man's eyes. Hardly the dynamo Nate had expected. He smoothed his longish brown hair away from his brow, rubbed his bearded cheek, then folded his hands in his lap. "I heard about Peter Jacks," he said, his gaze shifting between Nate and Gallant. His voice was soft, his speech hesitant.

"Did you know Jacks?"

"I never met him. But a couple of the counselors expressed concern about him. I guess he's been hanging around the facility with Jason Netters. What happened to Peter?"

"I'm afraid it's an ongoing investigation," Gallant said. "I can't really discuss it with you."

Denton shifted in his chair. "Sure, I can see that. Okay."

"Is there anything else?" Gallant asked.

Denton shrugged. "No, I don't think so. I…I just wanted to tell you you're welcome to come out and ask questions or take a look around—whatever. I mean, the fact he's been hanging out up there with us and then committed a crime, well, that could look bad, and you know, we depend on the community for support."

"I thought you were independently financed," Nate said.

"Sure. Yeah, we are. I mean, I am. I don't mean financial support. I mean as in goodwill."

"Oh, I see."

He wobbled a little as he stood. Gallant heaved himself upward in response. "Are you okay?"

Denton nodded. "I've had the flu," he said.

"Are you driving back up to the mountains tonight?" Gallant asked.

"No, I'm staying in town. I'll go back tomorrow. Don't worry about me. Good luck on your investigation."

The sheriff thanked Denton for coming in, then saw him out of the office. When he returned, he looked Nate straight in the eye. "What do you think of that?" he asked.

"Drugs?" Nate mused.

"I'm going to make sure the lab does a full toxicology on the Jacks boy. I've met Denton before, but the past five months haven't been kind to him. Sounds to me like an official visit is overdue up at that camp."

"That's just what Stew Netters said," Nate commented. As he left the office, he thought again about Jason Netters. Before he'd left the editor's office, Nate had made a point of greeting the boy. Jason had shaken his hand but hadn't made eye contact. But more than that, the kid had given the impression it was taking every ounce of his willpower to stay in that room and not spin away. He'd brought an undercurrent with him, or maybe his father had introduced it with that ill-advised comment about shooting Mike Donovan. All very odd, and Nate found himself wondering if the editor had any idea how troubled his boy seemed to be.

Nate tried Sarah's phone as he parked the rental in front of his motel room, but she didn't answer. To be on the safe side, he went inside the room to make sure she wasn't waiting for him, but the place smelled and looked as though it had recently been cleaned, and there was no sign that Sarah had been back there since before breakfast.

He knew she wasn't at the sheriff's office, so he veered toward the garage, thinking maybe she'd gone to get her stuff out of her mother's car, though why she wouldn't answer the phone if that was the case he didn't know.

The guy at the garage turned as Nate approached him. He was in the act of locking the front door and he winced when he saw Nate. "Oh, man, I was afraid you'd get back before she did," he said, pocketing his keys. "I gotta get home. I don't know what's taking her so long."

"Are we talking about Sarah Donovan?"

"Yeah. She wanted to run some errand or other, and since her car won't start, she asked to borrow your truck. She said she wouldn't be long, but it's been, like, three hours."

"Do you know where she went?" Nate asked.

"Out past the tunnel. Just two or three miles, she said."

"What's out that way?"

"Not much. A truck yard and an old mining operation.

Oh, and one of those storage places." He pulled his coat tighter around his thin frame and added, "My dad is going to kill me when he finds out I let her take your truck. I guess I shouldn't have, but I used to go to school with Sarah." He flashed a shy smile and added, "I had a thing for her, but she only had eyes for Johnny Pierce. Still, she's got a way about her."

"I know exactly what you mean," Nate said. "Don't worry about it. Did she take her suitcase out of her mother's car?"

"No. Did she want it?"

"Yeah. Mind getting it for me?"

"Not at all. Wait here. I'll go in through the garage door."

He trotted off, opened a small door behind the office and disappeared. He was back a few minutes later with Sarah's suitcase, which he handed to Nate.

NATE KEPT THINKING about that key Sarah had taken from her dad's safe. She'd explained it away by saying it concerned a personal matter. She'd also talked about a locker or garage her father rented in town. He had the gut feeling this personal matter concerned that storage locker and that she'd gone there to take care of something important to her. Reason said he should give her space to deal with whatever this was. He shouldn't intrude.

But on the other hand, she'd been gone far longer than she'd told the guy at the garage she would be, she was driving a truck with no window and it was getting dark. Plus, there was a storm coming. What if the truck had given her trouble?

Or what if another kind of trouble had come her way? There'd been so much violence in the past few days he couldn't rule anything out. In the end, he took off down the road.

U-Lock Garages was located 2.3 miles from town and was set down a slope from the highway. It was well lit with high overhead stanchions, and as the road passed it by, the whole thing could be seen from above. There wasn't a single vehicle visible on any of the honeycombed lanes, or a human, either, for that matter. Nate drove down to the gate, but it was locked and the office inside the gate looked empty and dark.

Sarah wasn't here.

He drove back toward town with his high beams on. About halfway through the tunnel, the lights revealed debris on the pavement and he slowed down. As the road was part of a blind curve at this point, he couldn't stop the truck on the off chance someone would come up behind him, despite the fact he hadn't met a single other car for at least a half mile. He drove out the tunnel and parked on the shoulder, grabbed a flashlight out of the center console and walked back into the tunnel.

The debris turned out to be broken red plastic from what looked like a taillight housing. He also saw the sparkle of glass. He swung the light in a circle and picked up what appeared to be a side mirror with a small convex mirror lens stuck to the only unbroken piece, just like the one he had mounted on his own vehicle to increase rearview visibility. Most of the mirror was shattered, which explained the glass.

He picked up the mirror and shined the light around again, and this time he saw white paint on the tunnel wall. That made his heart skip a beat. Running now, he headed for the opening, suddenly aware a vehicle was coming, its engine noise filling the tunnel. A second later, blinding lights came up behind him and passed with a blare of the horn that about shattered Nate's eardrums. He kept running, following the red taillights until they broke into the night and disappeared around another turn.

Using a flashlight to investigate the side of the road, he found tire tracks in the snow that careened down the slope. His hands and face were freezing by this time, and his lungs stung from taking deep breaths, but all that disappeared as he started down the slope, shining the light at his feet so he wouldn't trip and fall, noting the deep gouges and steamrolled bushes, until the light finally glinted off a silver bumper up ahead.

His white truck, all but invisible in the snow, appeared to have hit an old stump headfirst, popping the hood and stopping forward progress. Moving as fast as he could, Nate hurried to the driver's door and shined his light at the window, but not only was it tinted glass, it was also covered with condensation on the inside. He could tell someone was in there. He just couldn't see in what condition that someone might be. But it didn't take a rocket scientist to figure out who was behind the wheel.

He yanked on the handle. It was locked. He suddenly remembered he carried his keys in his pocket and swore at himself as he fumbled with numb fingers to find them and hit the auto lock button. The truck beeped and the door finally opened, triggering the cab light.

Sarah sat behind the wheel, staring at him as though she'd been asleep and had just woken. She still wore her seat belt. The deflated air bag extruding from the steering wheel covered most of her lap.

"Sarah," he said, touching her face, her shoulders, her arms, moving aside the air bag, looking for blood or jutting broken bones. She watched him in a distracted way until finally she whispered something.

He leaned closer. "What did you say, sweetheart?"

She licked her lips. "Sorry."

"Sorry about what?"

"Your truck."

"Don't worry about that," he said softly. "All that matters is you're okay. I'm calling the police and an ambulance."

She closed her eyes, but she'd slipped her hand into his and held on to him tightly. While they waited, Nate asked her if she hurt anywhere and she admitted her right leg ached. The crash had pushed the front end of the truck inward, pinning her inside, so there was no way he could check things out for her. He draped his coat across her body to ward off chattering teeth, held her hand and waited.

It seemed to take forever until he heard an approaching siren, but it was probably less than ten minutes. Searchlights appeared as another siren sounded off down the road. Pretty soon medics had pushed Nate aside and started attending to Sarah. When they were satisfied with her stability, the cops went to work freeing her from the mass of metal. Eventually she was transferred to a stretcher. Nate held her hand as they struggled up the hill until they reached the road and the welcome sight of the waiting ambulance.

Sheriff Gallant got out of his squad SUV. "That your truck down there?" he called to Nate.

"Yeah. Sarah was driving. She must have had an accident coming out of the tunnel."

Gallant looked down at Sarah, whose face was as white as the blanket tucked around her body. "Is she going to be okay?"

"Of course she is," Nate said, unable to entertain any other possibility.

But Sarah tugged on his hand. "Not an accident," she said.

Gallant heard her and both men leaned closer. "Then what?"

"Another truck. I went off the road."

"When did all this happen?" Nate asked.

"I looked at my watch a little while before. Around four o'clock."

The medics lifted the stretcher and Sarah disappeared into the back of the ambulance. Nate knew there wasn't room back there for unnecessary personnel, and he told Sarah he'd meet her at the hospital.

"You okay to drive?" Gallant asked.

Nate hurried to his rental. "Fine."

"I'll be by later to talk to her about this other vehicle," Gallant said.

"Fine," Nate repeated.

Gallant caught his arm. "Keep in mind it was *your* rental truck, and in the dark and from behind, no one could tell who was driving," he said.

Nate nodded. The number one important thing was Sarah's safety. Nate swore to himself. He wouldn't rest until he found out who had done this to her.

SARAH WAS EXTREMELY relieved when, after umpteen tests and X-rays, she was released from the hospital with little more than a mild concussion, a very sore neck and shoulders, and a sprained leg acquired when the truck floor pushed upward. She knew she was lucky to walk—well, limp—away from the crash and tried, as Nate drove toward the Motorcoach, to remember what had happened after the truck came to an abrupt standstill.

It was all blurry in her head, though. It had to have been a couple of hours that passed with her falling in and out of a strange slumber, growing colder and colder, unable to move herself out of the truck, always knowing in the back of her mind that Nate would look for her, Nate would find her, all she had to do was survive until he got there.

She hadn't been able to tell the sheriff much about the other vehicle except it was a truck slightly bigger than Nate's and dark in color. Judging from his deep sigh, she assumed that description fit a whole lot of Shatter-horn's vehicles. She did point out that it was likely to have suffered damage on the right side when it had slammed against Nate's truck. She hadn't seen the driver, hadn't even tried to as she'd been struggling with the steering wheel in an attempt to avoid what eventually happened.

"How are you doing over there?" Nate asked, his hand coming to rest atop hers.

"Worried about tomorrow," she said. "Worried that we're going to hear there's been a senseless shooting at the Washington Monument and that more innocent people are going to die and we don't know how to stop it. Did you call your department in Arizona?"

"Yeah, while you were in X-ray. I talked to Dan. He promised to pass on the word to his brother. He tried to assure me that the FBI would be on top of any conspiracy, domestic or foreign."

"That's what everyone says," Sarah remarked as they pulled into the motel parking lot.

As Nate unlocked the door, his cell phone rang. In a way, he hated to answer it. It was late, both he and Sarah were exhausted, and there just wasn't anyone he wanted to talk to except the person or persons behind what was going on, and he doubted they would phone to explain themselves.

"Go ahead and take that call," Sarah said, dropping her handbag on the bedside table and heading to the bathroom.

He dropped into the chair by the small desk and saw on

the screen that it was Gallant. "What are you doing still up?" he asked in lieu of a greeting.

"Acting like your darn answering machine. First Diana Donovan called, supposedly to hear what we'd found out about her ex-husband's murder, but I got the feeling she really wanted to find out where Sarah was."

"Okay," Nate said. "And speaking of Sarah, what kind of vehicle does Netters drive? And how about his son? And the mayor, too. And Morris Denton."

"Let's see. Netters drives a dark green four-door truck. George Bliss has a white car and a dark truck. Jason drives his dad's old—wait for it—truck. I don't know about Denton, but he was in my office with you when Sarah was run off the road." He paused a second. "Besides, why would any of them run your truck off the road?"

"I don't know," Nate admitted.

"There's something else," the sheriff continued. "Jessica Foster has been trying to get ahold of you. She finally called my office, and they called me, and I called her and promised I'd pass along a message. She wants to talk to you right away, no matter what time it is."

"Do you know what this is about?" Nate asked.

"I'll let her explain," Gallant said and smothered a yawn. Nate thanked him and clicked off his phone, then clicked it back on and called the Foster house.

Jessica picked it up before the ringtone finished. "Nate? Is that you?"

"Yeah," he said. "I tried calling last night and left a message—"

"You did? I must have erased it or something. Oh, Nate, Alex is missing!"

"Missing?"

"No one has seen or heard from him since the day he flew out of here. The last communication put him over the mountains during that storm. As soon as the weather cleared, they started a search, but there's nothing. Nothing!"

"Wait a second," Nate said. "What about the aircraft's emergency beacon?"

"Nothing," she insisted. "Absolutely no trace. You know how he likes his old equipment and refuses to update. And now another storm is brewing, so they have to call off tomorrow's search, and he's out there in the cold—" Her voice broke off while she excused herself and blew her nose, then she was back, a little calmer but not much. "We had a big argument before he left, Nate. I told him not to bother coming home. What if those are the last words I ever say to him?"

Nate took a deep breath. Alex was his best friend, so Nate knew about the occasional arguments. Money was tight at times; in-laws were an issue; his work was demanding. Hers was, too. They both wanted children and yet had struggled conceiving…. Things almost everyone had trouble with at times. But Nate hadn't known things had gotten this bad between Alex and his wife.

After a long hesitation, she spoke again. "I'm just going to blurt this out, Nate. Maybe Alex disarmed his own beacon. Maybe he decided to cut his losses with me and start fresh."

"No," Nate said. "He wouldn't do it this way."

"How do you know? He's a detective in the Blunt Falls police department—if anyone could figure out how to disappear, it would be Alex."

"He wouldn't bail on you or his career or his family," Nate insisted, hoping with all his heart he was right.

"You never know what really goes on with people," she said, her voice ragged, tired. "You can know them so well and yet not know them at all. Anyway, I didn't want you to find out he was missing on the news or read it in a paper."

"I appreciate that," Nate said.

"Sheriff Gallant told me that Mike Donovan is dead. 'Murdered,' he said. Nate, what's the world coming to?"

Nate had no pithy reassurance to offer. His head was reeling with the images of Alex crashed, injured, helpless in the bitterly cold mountains. "Are you alone?" he asked Jessica just as Sarah emerged from the bathroom wrapped in a towel, damp hair clinging to her beautiful face. She limped over to the bed and perched on the edge, staring at him. Apparently the tone of his voice and the urgency of the conversation had alerted her to his distress.

"My sister is here. I'm okay. How about you, Nate?"

"I'll come as soon as I can," he said. "We'll find him."

"I hope so," Jessica responded, and she just seemed to fade away.

Nate quickly filled Sarah in on the details, explaining he would leave for Montana the day after tomorrow. She nodded thoughtfully, then winced as the movement apparently hurt her strained muscles. "What a horrible coincidence," she said, rubbing her neck with one hand.

He got up and approached her. "Let me do that," he said. "Come sit in the chair."

She sat down in his vacated chair and he gently began massaging her neck and shoulders, delighting in the petal softness of her skin and the pure beauty of her back. But even while he enjoyed the scenery, he found himself thinking, at first to himself and then aloud.

"Is it a coincidence?" he said, trying out the words.

"It has to be," she responded. "How could it be anything else? I mean, one man is shot and another's plane disappears. The only thing they had in common—"

"—was a shooting they were part of in Shatterhorn, Nevada, months before. And me."

She grabbed his hand and pulled him around to face her. He sat on the bed so she wouldn't have to strain herself to look up at him. "And someone's been trying to kill you since that same day," she said.

"I've been thinking about something that happened outside of Vegas when I was on my way up here. One of my tires blew on a nasty piece of highway. At the time, there was a lot of dust blowing across the road, so I'd slowed way down, and traffic was relatively light. I remember thinking had I been going the speed limit or if traffic had been heavier, the resulting crash and repairs might have been a whole lot worse. As it was, it delayed me by two or three hours."

"So now you're thinking it wasn't an accident?"

"In light of everything else, yes. I'd stopped for a late breakfast at a real busy truck stop because I'd left home at the crack of dawn. I was there about twenty-five minutes. The tire blew five miles down the road."

"I'm getting chills," Sarah said, hugging herself.

"If I'm right, that means Mike, Alex and I were all targeted on the same day, which just happens to be right after Mike asked us to meet him here. Both the editor and the mayor heard Mike say he was asking us to come and who knows how many people they told. I think from what I've heard since then that your father was shut down by so many people he was getting desperate to be heard. He thought he saw a pattern, but he was too mixed-up in his thinking. He thought something horrible was coming tomorrow."

She nodded and winced again.

He looked at her closely. She was shivering and pale, and he was suddenly ashamed he hadn't insisted she spend the night in the hospital. But how could he protect her there? Time was running out and their enemy was faceless. The attack on Sarah had changed the stakes. "I retrieved your suitcase from the garage before I found you," he said. "I'll go get it out of the truck. You need something warmer than that towel."

"Don't go," she said.

He took her hands and pulled her to her feet. The action jarred loose the towel and his breath caught as it slipped to the floor. "And your mother tried calling you today," he added around the sudden lump in his throat.

"My phone is dead and the charger unit is in my suitcase."

"I'll go get it."

"Not now," she said. "It's a car charger. Anyway, I'm very tired." She rested her head against his shoulder. "I don't need to talk to my mother right now, and I certainly don't need clothes to stay warm—not when I have you."

He picked her up in his arms and held her, kissing her soft lips as he gently laid her down on the bed. A few minutes later, they were under the sheets, making heat of their own. When they finally parted, Sarah fell asleep almost at once, but Nate lay awake, staring into the dark, thinking....

He kept picturing the last page in Mike's notebook. A big number twenty-eight circled in red ink.

A cold fist seemed to punch him in the gut as his brain ran through dates and months until he reached May. What day was Memorial Day on this year?

He'd bet it was the twenty-eighth.

Had Mike suspected another shooting would occur in late May?

Chapter Fifteen

Sarah woke up first. She must have groaned when she rolled on her side, because Nate's arms suddenly surrounded her. She could tell he'd fallen back to sleep when his breathing once again turned slow and steady.

Her handbag lay on the bedside table, and carefully, so as not to awaken Nate, she reached inside for Johnny's letters.

Nate's embrace tightened. She left the letters where they were and turned in the circle of his arms to kiss him awake.

"Morning breath," he warned her without opening his eyes.

"I'll take my chances," she said, giving him a chaste kiss.

"How are you? How do you feel?"

"Fine," she said. "Antsy."

"Me, too," he said as though coming fully awake, and she could sense him thinking: this was *the day*. What exactly that meant might still elude both of them, but there was no denying the relentless feeling something was going to happen soon. This was the day the country celebrated its presidents both past and present. Sarah hoped Nate's buddy Dan had made more headway figuring this out than her father had.

Nate disengaged himself and got out of bed, walking to the bathroom in that sure-footed way of his, totally at ease with his body. There was no reason why he shouldn't be. The man was built perfectly, muscles defined without bulging, good health exuding through his pores. She was still staring at him as he looked back from the bathroom door and winked at her.

Eventually, Nate retrieved her suitcase from the truck cab and they made it into their clothes. Then Nate called his friend Alex's wife for an update, and from the stoic look on his face and the paucity of conversation, Sarah could tell nothing had changed. She was unsure why he asked the woman to consult a calendar, or why he nodded as she spoke.

"Alex is still missing," he said. "And according to Jessica, Memorial Day falls on the twenty-eighth of May this year, as in the number twenty-eight circled in red ink. It makes sense something would happen on that date, as it ties in with all the other shootings on similar holidays."

"Of course," Sarah said.

He handed her the phone. "Your turn."

It was obvious Sarah's early-morning call had awakened her night-owl mother from a sound sleep. She hung up after five minutes of hedging to find Nate staring at her.

"What's up?" he asked.

"She apologized for going to the bar. She wants me to come back to Reno. She wants to talk to me."

"And?" he said.

"And I've heard it all before." She cupped her forehead and closed her eyes for a minute. "I told her I'd come when I could. Let's get some breakfast."

"How about I bring something back from the motel office and we eat it here?"

"That sounds good," she said and laid her head back

against the chair. A second later she heard the door close and lock behind him. "Come on, painkiller," she whispered.

It felt good to be back in jeans and a sweater, although she'd had to trash her boots after the medics cut apart the right one to remove it from her injured leg. She'd brought along running shoes and laced the right one gingerly. As she waited for Nate to return, she thought about going to the nightstand and getting Johnny's letter, but her leg hurt and she just wanted to sit still. Five minutes later, she heard a noise at the door as though Nate was having trouble opening it, maybe because his hands were full. It wasn't until she swung it open that the thought crossed her mind—what if it wasn't Nate?

But it was, and he entered the room in a rush. It was obvious by his expression something was wrong. He closed the door and slid the deadbolt, turning to look at her.

"Now what?" she asked, her heart suddenly racing.

"Stewart Netters is dead."

Sarah stared at him a second. "Jason's father? The editor of the *Shatterhorn Gazette?*"

"The motel management had the television on. He was shot sometime early this morning."

"Poor Jason."

"They're looking for Jason in connection with his father's death," Nate interrupted. "Someone saw him leaving the newspaper office in a dead run. They interviewed the sheriff's department."

By this time, Sarah had turned on the set in their room and found the Reno news station covering the story. A woman's anguished face filled the screen. Sarah looked up at Nate. "That's Giselle Netters, Jason's mother."

"Turn it up," Nate urged.

"I don't believe it, not for a minute, not any of it," Giselle was saying. "Jason would never, ever do something like this.

He loves his father. He would never hurt him. Stew couldn't sleep last night—he was troubled about something—so he went in early to the office. The sheriff's department has this all wrong, I swear. They should be looking for the person who murdered my husband, not wasting time trying to make a case against our son. Jason, please, if you can hear me, come home…."

Her tear-streaked face was replaced by that of an anchorwoman sporting rigidly coiffed red hair. "You've been listening to the alleged attacker's mother, Giselle Netters, wife of shooting victim Stewart Netters. Mr. Netters's body was discovered early this morning by an employee. He'd been shot once in the chest with what sources claim is a .380. Shatterhorn mayor George Bliss was unavailable for comment."

The newswoman paused before adding in a more modulated voice, "Viewers will remember the small community of Shatterhorn faced another disaster just last Labor Day, when a nineteen-year-old gunman by the name of Thomas Jacks injured five and killed four in a crowded mall before turning his weapon on himself. And in a strange twist of fate, the man who was with Jacks as he took his dying breath was shot and killed three days ago by an unknown assailant. Speculation is growing that perhaps Jason Netters was involved with that shooting, as well. In other news…"

"Turn it off, please," Nate said.

Sarah was happy to do as he'd requested. For a moment they both sat there staring at each other, and then Sarah took a steadying breath. "Maybe this is it," she said. "Maybe it's over."

"What do you mean?" Nate asked her.

"Dad speculated something would happen on Presidents' Day, and it has."

"I don't think so," Nate said.

"There are similarities," she insisted. "A shooting committed by a young man—"

"But not random," Nate interrupted. "A son killing his father is never random. And Jason didn't then kill himself—he apparently fled. If he's guilty. If he did this."

Sarah, feeling deflated, nodded. As horrible as this recent event was, she'd experienced a few moments of pure relief—the worst was over at last. But now she could see there was no way to know that, not until they found Jason.

"Are you hungry?" he asked her.

"Not anymore."

"Me, neither. Let's drive over to the mayor's house and ask him what happened in Netters's office yesterday after I left. Maybe he's not making a public comment because he has information the sheriff doesn't want him to reveal."

"Would he tell us?"

"Probably not, but even knowing he has something might help and maybe Gallant would share. It's someplace to start."

They left the room soon after that, pleased to see the weather system that had appeared so threatening the night before had barely dusted the streets with snow. Both of them were on the quiet side. In an abstract way, Sarah recognized the care with which Nate checked the cars behind them, the pedestrians on the street, his eyes constantly scanning everyone and everything as though he was looking for a killer.

Perhaps that was because he was.

IT WAS OBVIOUS to Nate that Mayor George Bliss lived in a style befitting his family's wealth, from the locked rod-iron gates at the head of the curving driveway to the white mansion visible inside the fenced grounds. An American flag, beautiful against the grayish sky, waved above the roof. A call box sat next to the gate complete with a video monitor, which Nate got out of the truck and activated.

A decisive voice he recognized from a phone call made a couple of days before responded. The image showed a balding man with a prominent, thin nose. "Yes?"

"I'm here to see Mayor Bliss," Nate said.

The man looked annoyed as he said, "You media people have been told over and over again that the mayor isn't giving statements right now."

"I'm not with the media," Nate said, giving his name. "And you are?"

"The mayor's secretary, William Tucker. I'm sorry, sir, but I was just leaving. If you'll try again tomorrow—"

Nate tried out a smile. "Mr. Tucker, I need to ask Mayor Bliss a couple of quick questions."

The man's irritated frown curved a little. "Are you the Nate Matthews who was at the mall last Labor Day?"

"That's me."

"I see. Nevertheless, the message is the same. The mayor is indisposed."

"In what way?"

"Sir, in deference to the high regard in which the mayor holds you and your friends, I will tell you what I haven't divulged to the media. Mayor Bliss is not presently in Shatterhorn."

"Can you tell me where he is?"

For a moment, it appeared a challenging glint flared in the man's eyes. "He flew out this morning for Helena. I'm not supposed to advertise that information, so please don't share it. The mayor and Mr. Netters were good friends. This horrible...event...has hit him hard."

"May I ask what he's doing in Helena?"

"He's attending a Presidents' Day celebration to show support for the governor. He agreed to go just last night."

Presidents' Day. "Okay. Well, thanks for your time."

"Come back tomorrow morning," the man said curtly. "I'll make sure the mayor is expecting you."

Nate got back in the truck and faced Sarah, who had leaned her head against the window and closed her eyes. She looked delicate and beaten, her face a little black-and-blue, her lips pale. He swallowed a knot as she opened her eyes and met his gaze. "Well?"

"Bliss isn't here," he told her, his voice choked. What was he doing with this woman? She was hurt; she should be home in bed. If he truly cared for her, would he keep dragging her into danger? Wouldn't he insist she go back to Reno or Virginia, where it was safe, instead of subjecting her to this awful series of violent situations that just never seemed to stop?

Because it was suddenly very clear to him that the situation with her mother, while volatile, had never put Sarah's life in imminent danger. He and Mike had brought the violence, and it was still following Nate around like a very cruel shadow. Sarah was a victim every bit as much as her father, and all Nate had done was replace her needy mother with his own needs. True to form, Sarah had followed that misguided sense of loyalty that seemed inherent to her soul and almost died because of it. Again.

He cleared his throat. "I'm going to take you back to the motel, where I hope you'll lock yourself in the room and not answer the door unless it's for food you ordered yourself."

Her eyes widened. "Where are you going?"

He told her about Helena as he started the truck. "Do you know where it is?"

"A couple of hours driving, far less by plane," she said.

"What about the roads? If the storm dumped snow, they could be impassable." Unbidden, he pictured Alex lost in those mountains, freezing, hurt.

"No, they should be fine. It's not a bad drive." She narrowed her eyes. "*Why* are you going to Helena?"

"To see the mayor."

"But why? The chances you'll even be able to get close to him seem remote, and you said he'll be back by tonight."

"Tonight I'm going up to that B-Strong camp."

"Why?"

"I want to get a feel for the place, because tomorrow I need to drive to Blunt Falls to see what I can do to help find Alex."

She was quiet for a second. "I can't leave tomorrow. I have to take care of moving the coins and contacting a lawyer."

"I know," he agreed. "And your mother wants you back in Reno."

She looked down at her hands, then at him. "What are you really saying, Nate?"

He paused for a second, measuring his words. "I'm saying maybe it's time we each took care of business. You have your family. I have this."

"Do you?" she asked.

"What do you mean?"

"Why can't you let the police take care of it?"

"That's not the way I work."

"You're beginning to sound like my father."

His mouth opened, but no words came out. He wasn't even sure what they were fighting about, only that her accusation hurt like salt rubbed in an open wound. After several seconds of tense stillness, he muttered, "When you've been in law enforcement as long as I have, you get a sixth sense about things."

"You're talking about a gut feeling," she said. "What is your gut telling you?"

"That the mayor is in danger."

"From Jason?"

"I'm not sure. But he and Stewart were both in Jason's father's office yesterday, and Jason is hiding something. I can guarantee you that. It's worth a drive to Helena and that's why I have to go. But there's no reason for you to tag along."

"No need for me to tag along?" she repeated, obviously annoyed. "Well, it's not that easy. This isn't just about you, Nate."

"I didn't say it was."

"Didn't you? I'm going, too."

"Sarah—"

"Don't you know by now that there is no point arguing with me?"

"That's kind of scary, isn't it?"

"I'm usually pretty reasonable," she objected, her voice dry.

"No, I mean it's kind of scary that I know that about you." He glanced at her as he said this and his expression struck her as uneasy.

"I see your point," she said softly. "But isn't it kind of nice, too?"

"Yeah," he said, but it came with a quick turn of his head and, after that, utter silence.

SARAH CLOSED HER EYES, drifting in and out of restless slumber. Nate had the heat turned up and that felt good, because everything hurt more today than it had the day before.

Why was he acting so odd? How had he gone from the lover of the night before to this hard-to-read, all-too-typical guy? Was it her fault? And why had she insisted on accompanying him when it was clear he'd rather she didn't? In the back of her mind, she asked herself a question: Was it possible she'd made the error of mistaking sex for genuine feeling? Mistaking passion for compassion?

Or was Nate rediscovering his old self, the cop under his skin, and with that, his swagger? And if that were true, perhaps it was also possible he was beginning to reexamine his severed relationship with his fiancée. Perhaps letting her go now seemed a huge mistake he needed to rectify.

She dug in her purse when they stopped for gas and Nate got out to stretch his legs. The whole stack of Johnny's letters came out and with it, a much folded and unfolded piece of paper she recognized as having been wrapped around the storage-garage key. She was about to stuff it back in her handbag when she saw writing on one side.

"What's that?" Nate asked as he climbed back in behind the wheel of the rental.

"A name. Morris Denton, with *Seattle* written under it followed by a question mark. What do you suppose that means?"

"Is that the missing page from the notebook?"

"It looks like it. It was wrapped around the key I found in Dad's safe. I'm so stupid. I should have recognized it, but this is the first time I really looked at it." She handed the paper to Nate.

"I have no idea why he'd include Seattle unless Denton is from there or was going there. We'll get Gallant to check on it tonight." He gestured at the letters still in her lap. "What are those?"

She looked him in the eyes. "Johnny wrote me these before we were married."

"That's what you went to the garage to get," he said.

"Yes. I wanted to read them again."

"You really loved him, didn't you?" he asked her.

She nodded. "I really did. I'm funny that way. When I give my heart, I give my heart."

"I'm sorry I pried," he said, starting the truck, and from the tone of his voice, it was clear the letters held little interest for him. Sarah took a deep breath and thanked her lucky stars. If he'd asked why they were important to her, she would have told him, and now was not the time—not when things had gotten so strange between them. She stuffed the letters back in her purse right as a road sign announced Helena just ahead.

Chapter Sixteen

The town of Helena was home to a small college, which considerably boosted its wintertime population. And on this chilly Monday afternoon, the one-way street leading into town was jammed with traffic. Even the sidewalks were crowded, and everyone moved in the same direction toward the center of town.

"This is Union Street," Sarah announced as they crawled along. "It leads to Memorial Plaza, and if I remember correctly from the one and only time I've ever been here, there's a big old statue of George Washington right smack in the middle. I never put the two together before."

"Washington Memorial," Nate whispered, his gut sending signals again. "This is it. Something is going to happen here." He stopped for a group of people who were crossing the street and added, "Where is everybody going?"

"Judging from the red-white-and-blue banners, I'd say a parade or something. Look, the road is blocked off up ahead."

Nate followed behind a trolley until he saw a sign directing him to a makeshift parking lot and pulled out of the traffic. "We'd better walk from here," he said as he turned off the engine. "Are you up to it? Maybe you should stay in the truck."

"Why do you keep trying to get rid of me?" she snapped. "What's gotten into you?"

"I don't want you to get killed," he grumbled as he slipped Mike's old leather notebook into the breast pocket of his jacket. He wasn't proud of the childish way his emotions were getting the best of him. If something happened to her that he could prevent and he somehow missed the mark, like he had on Labor Day with those kids, he'd never forgive himself. He'd never make it back to anything approaching normal. For both their sakes, he wanted to park her in a steel vault until this was over.

"I'm a big girl, Nate," she said as she took his hand, clenching it in hers and tugging slightly for effect. He stopped to look down at her, but the crowd swept them up and they moved with everyone else toward the town square.

Helena's elevation was lower than Shatterhorn's, hence the pavement was clear of snow and nearly empty. As they staked out a piece of curbside real estate, a chill wind carried the sound of an approaching brass band. Across the road, Nate could see the grassy square and the top of Washington's head. His pulse raced as he looked for anything amiss.

Within minutes, everyone seemed to turn in unison to watch the distant corner with murmurs of expectation. As the music grew louder, two brown quarter horses made the turn, their riders carrying the state and national flags.

The crowd cheered as the horses, followed by the Helena High School Tigers band, pranced by. A float complete with three young women draped in period clothes topped with fur coats, as well as two guys dressed as Abraham Lincoln and George Washington, came after the band. The girls waved like prom queens while the guys looked embarrassed and cold. A dozen or so kids riding decorated bikes and so bundled in parkas their own mothers probably couldn't tell them apart followed the float. A half dozen brave girls in brief uniforms twirling batons preceded the next float, which featured a seated woman hand sewing the Stars and Stripes—à la Betsy Ross—onto a huge flag. Every so often she reached into a sack and threw a handful of candy to the kids.

Nate grew increasingly anxious. This was exactly the kind of venue these "random" shooters had been choosing—crowded, everyday Americana events, complete with families and celebration, as though the whole point was to underscore that no one was safe, not at school or in a library or on a beach. He looked back at the parade as an open car drove by. Two men were seated in the backseat, and by the banners affixed to the door, Nate figured out one was the mayor of Helena and the other was the governor of Nevada. Nate was kind of surprised Bliss wasn't in the car with them.

He tore his gaze away from the men and went back to scanning the crowd. A few minutes later, his heart leaped into his throat as he recognized a face in among the strangers.

He grabbed Sarah's arm, propelling her forward with him lest he lose sight of his target. "Go get the police."

"Why?"

He tore his gaze away from the opposite side of the street. "I just saw Jason Netters. I have to follow him." Nate began walking again, aware Sarah was close behind. He apologized to an older woman as he sidled past her, moving faster than the parade now, out in front of the horses in an effort not to lose sight of Jason.

"I'm coming with you."

He glanced down at her again. "Go find help," he pleaded.

"Tell them anything you can think of to get this crowd dispersed. I have to keep up with Jason."

"Where's he going? Can you tell?"

"It looks like he's headed to the end of the parade route."

He ran off, not pausing to look back. He had to find Jason and stop him before it was too late.

SARAH LOOKED AROUND desperately for someone in a uniform, and when she finally spotted an officer working crowd control, she hurried to speak to him, her leg throbbing in protest.

The man was several inches taller than she was, and the noise of the crowd drowned out her voice. Plus, he was involved in another situation and was only paying her cursory attention. When he turned the opposite direction to control a horde of little kids, she grabbed his arm, and he turned to face her, annoyed now that she'd interfered with him.

"A guy wanted for questioning in the shooting death of a man in Shatterhorn this morning has been sighted on his way to the end of the parade," she explained breathlessly. "Is there a gathering down there?"

"Yeah," he said, shooing the kids back.

"Get on your radio and tell the others to be alert. There's reason to suspect this person is armed and might be getting ready to fire into the crowd."

"Are you serious?" he asked.

"Dead serious."

"What's his name?"

"Jason Netters. About eighteen, blond, medium sized."

"That describes two-thirds of this town," he said, but he was fingering his radio as he spoke. "And who are you?"

"It doesn't matter who I am. Please, do something. I have to go."

A CONGESTED BARRICADE at the end of the sidewalk directing pedestrians to cross the street and continue down toward a park Nate could see through the trees caused him to lose sight of Jason. He crossed with everyone else, keeping his gaze peeled for a glimpse of the boy, but Jason wasn't a big guy and he wasn't particularly distinctive.

Wait—he'd been wearing a green camouflage-type coat. Those were hardly rare in rural Nevada, but at least it gave Nate something to be on the lookout for.

Checking the street, he saw the parade was now making its way to the park, where bleachers were beginning to fill with people. He, along with two dozen others, got stuck behind the last float, and by the time Nate made it to the park, the car with the dignitaries had come to a halt. The governor and Helena's mayor were in the process of climbing up to a platform where a podium had been situated. There was no sign of Mayor Bliss, which seemed odd. The band launched into another march song and people cheered. The noise and confusion made concentrating that much harder. Where was Jason?

He caught a glimpse of the back of a head covered with straw-colored hair and took off after him. Three minutes later, he touched the guy's shoulder. A man spun around and raised his eyebrows. He was ten years too old. "Something wrong, pal?" he asked.

"Sorry," Nate said. He made his way back to the bandstand and climbed up three or four levels. Since the park sat on a slight incline from the town, it gave a panoramic view of things. Nate scanned the almost deserted streets and saw nothing and no one suspicious. Turning his head, he caught traffic and a glimpse of movement headed toward a freeway underpass not too far away. He kept staring until two figures emerged from some deep shadows and came briefly into view before disappearing again.

One guy had buzz-cut silver hair and wore a long coat; the other one wore a camouflage jacket. The mayor and Jason walking together, Jason's hand on the mayor's arm as though forcing him to come along, the mayor's gait stiff and labored.

Nate jumped off the bleachers and started winding his way out of the park in the general direction of the freeway, his eyes peeled for some sign that Sarah had managed to find a cop. No such luck. For a second, he thought about returning to the stands to warn people, but warn them about what? If Jason's goal was to conduct a random shooting into the crowd, he wouldn't be taking the mayor the opposite direction, would he? And panicking a large group of people could lead to a stampede and trampling.

For about the fortieth time since leaving Arizona, Nate wished he'd kept his badge and his gun. Who had he been trying to kid? He was who and what he was—a deputy, plain and simple. He didn't want to sit behind a desk as sheriff. He didn't want to spend his life hiding on his ranch. He just wanted to be a decent lawman again, but this going at it through the back door was crazy. At least Sarah wasn't in the middle of it for a change, and that was something to be thankful for.

The noise of the crowd behind him quickly began to fade, but traffic picked up and cars sped by on the road to his left. Nate stopped running after a few minutes in order to slow down and look around. Where had the two men gone?

The sky had clouded over, the shadows under the overpass ahead deep and dark. Nate stopped altogether and stood with his back against a signpost, listening. A car whizzed by followed by another car, and as the noise of their engines drifted away, Nate heard a voice coming from the dark part of the overpass.

"Come to your senses, son," the mayor said, his tone reasonable and calm. "Shooting me won't bring back your father."

"I'm not your *son*," Jason said. In contrast to the mayor's voice, the boy's reply was raspy and raw with emotion.

Nate peered into the gloom and saw the flash of metal. There were two men in there. How did he approach them? They'd see and hear him the moment he got closer.

Headlights coming from the other direction were mounted high enough to announce they belonged to a large semi-truck. Nate looked off to his right and glimpsed a subtle path etched into the dirt leading up the embankment and under the overpass. He pictured a shelf of sorts where people with nowhere better to be waited out rain and snow. Using the roaring noise of the approaching truck as cover, he scrambled up the dirt trail, and sure enough, erupted onto a narrow ledge littered with cast-off garbage. He hunkered down and considered his options.

He was now directly above the two men, whose voices were still drowned out by the sound of the retreating truck. They were standing on a very wide sidewalk, facing each other. Jason was holding a gun close to his own body, pointed at the mayor's chest.

Nate knew he had one chance to get this right. He had to throw himself down the ten feet of slope, hit Jason dead-on and knock the gun out of his hand. He knew the moment the kid became aware of Nate's presence, instinct would guide his next move. He would turn his weapon and fire without hesitation.

"You don't get it, do you?" the mayor was saying as Nate's muscles bunched in his legs.

"I get it," Jason said. "I just don't want any more. I can't do it." He reached out and shoved the mayor, who stumbled backward.

Another car was coming, and once again, Nate used the distraction to cover himself. He started down the slope. When he saw Jason's head begin to turn, he launched himself into the air. A second later, he collided with the boy, who folded under the impact of Nate's body.

For a second, they struggled, then Nate wrangled away the gun. He stood, keeping the kid under cover, breathing heavy from exertion and adrenaline. His hat had flown off in the attack and lay in the middle of the road. The mayor had stumbled backward after Jason's shove and now stared at the boy, his face red beneath the tan, his eyes all but popping out of his head, the tendons in his neck bulging.

"You okay?" Nate hollered as a car roared by, its tires flattening his hat.

The mayor limped toward him, heavily favoring his right leg. With a start, Nate realized this was the first time he'd seen the man stand since getting to town. "Thanks to you," he said.

"Stop him!" Jason shouted, still on the ground.

Nate's brow furled. "'Stop him'? What are you talking about?"

"He shot my dad," Jason said, sitting up now, holding his head.

"You can't believe that," Bliss said. "The boy is obviously crazy."

"I'm not," Jason said, and for the first time this trip, he met Nate's gaze with his own. He got to his feet, lurching a little, unsteady, rubbing his chin, then he turned his attention to the mayor. "You shot Dad because I told him who you really are. He went to work early. He said he was going to call you and demand you come talk to him. And you shot him, you bastard!"

The mayor looked at Nate's hand. "Give me his gun."

Nate clutched the weapon tighter. "The police will show up here sooner or later. We'll let them figure this out."

"This isn't any of your business," Bliss said.

Nate glanced at Jason again. "What exactly did you tell your father?"

It took Jason a few moments to speak. Tears streamed down his face and his voice trembled. "Dad said he was going up to B-Strong to interview Morris Denton. I told him the truth. Horrible things."

"You're not making sense," the mayor said. He'd moved to within four feet of Nate and Jason.

"Morris is a doper," Jason said.

"Watch what you say about people," Bliss hissed.

"You really run the camp," Jason continued, his voice icy calm. "You choose people to do what you want. You chose me. Today was my turn. I was supposed to shoot into the crowd, keep my bullets low so little kids would get it in the head and adults in the gut. You said—"

The mayor struck fast, hitting Jason in the face with his fist, knocking the boy to the ground. The action jarred Bliss's body and he wheeled away. A truck drove by and Nate caught a momentary glance of startled faces. No doubt they thought there was some sort of drunken brawl going on. Good—maybe they'd call the police.

"What the hell is going on?" Nate demanded of both of them.

"The boy is off his rocker," the mayor said, wiping spit from his chin with his fist. "Give me his gun and I'll take him back into town."

Nate reached down to grab Jason's arm and haul him to his feet. Another car sped by.

"Ask him how he hurt his leg," Jason said.

"You shoved me," Bliss spat.

The image of the two men walking away from the park flashed in Nate's mind. "You were walking funny way before Jason shoved you," he said.

"That's because you shot him," Jason said, looking at Nate. "That's why he sent Peter after you and now Peter is dead just like his brother." Jason once again glared at the mayor as he added, "You called us your foot soldiers, but the truth is we were your puppets."

"What are you talking about?" Nate asked, but he knew. *He knew.*

"It's him, don't you see? He's got this crazy idea that if people are afraid all the time, they'll fight to keep men like him in power. They'll oppose gun laws. He uses their fear. He finds guys who are troubled or weak—"

"I'm not going to stand here while this brat slanders me," Bliss sneered. "Put a bullet in him and save the taxpayers the cost of paying for his trial."

At that moment, someone touched Nate's shoulder and he turned to find Sarah facing him. He'd been so involved in what was going on, he hadn't heard her approach. She looked positively worn-out, pale and breathless.

"Where are the cops?" he asked her, wishing with all his heart she hadn't arrived at that moment.

"They must still be in the park. Someone said they saw a tall man in a hat run off this way, so I followed, and then I heard yelling, so I hurried. Nate, what's going on?"

Nate took a chance he understood everything correctly. "Jason, run back to the park. Get the police to come out here. Don't tell them your name or they'll stop to arrest you and there's no time. Go now and hurry." He wanted to send Sarah with the boy, but he didn't think she had speed in her right that moment.

In a flash, Jason was running back to the park. His exit

created just enough chaos for the mayor to take advantage of the distraction. Once again moving way faster than Nate anticipated, the older man grabbed Sarah and pulled her against his chest, his arm moving up to circle her throat. "Give me that gun," he growled, "or I push her in front of the next car that comes by."

"It's too late. It's over," Nate said, looking for a way to shoot the mayor without hitting Sarah. There just wasn't one. "You killed Mike. You must have taken his computer and phone, and then when I called him, you listened to the message and knew I was in town, that I'd survived that near accident down by Vegas. Did you pay someone to sabotage my car? And why kill Mike? Did he figure out your involvement in the B-Strong camp? What the hell were you doing out there? Recruiting gunmen to sacrifice for your own agenda?"

"You have no idea how many of us there are," Bliss growled. "I'm just one man, but there are others all over the country. The malcontent losers we choose are all on a one-way bus to nowhere. We have to stay vigilant. This is not the time for restraint and caution. This is the time to fight back, to take control. I gave those boys' deaths a meaning."

"And the innocent people they killed?"

"Every single one of them died for their countrymen. What greater honor?"

"You are a warped, twisted man," Nate said, Bliss's claim there were more like him a chilling thought. But how else could they attack Hawaii and Nevada and Iowa and heaven knew where else? "You're hiding behind the flag and corrupting the very ideals you say you stand for. You don't want people to be free to make choices. You want to decide for them. You followed us to Carson City, you ran Sarah off the road, and what the hell did you or someone like you do to Alex's plane?"

"Mike Donovan was a miserable little weasel. He poked around and poked around. I had to stop him. He would have ruined everything. And you and your buddy are no better." He took a deep breath and lowered his voice. "We're not going to talk anymore. One last time, Matthews. The gun for the girl."

"Don't do it," Sarah said as a car raced by. A big truck was right behind the car. Bliss yanked Sarah closer to the street. He smiled at Nate and pushed her with abandon. Sarah stumbled backward toward death. The truck blared a horn, swerved and kept going, but another car was on its heels. Nate grabbed for Sarah with one hand. Her fingers slipped from his and he dropped the gun in his effort to grip both her wrists. He was vaguely aware of the screech of brakes. For one second, Sarah's terrified eyes stared into his, then he pulled with everything he could muster. They both rolled to the pavement as the car continued on its way. Sarah must have hit her head. Her eyes were closed and her body was limp. Nate struggled to his feet and quickly pulled her body to the sidewalk, lifting her to safety just as another car went by.

When he looked up he found exactly what he'd expected to find—the gun was gone and George Bliss was running away from town, practically dragging his injured leg in his rush to escape. Nate took off after him. Bliss turned, took aim and fired.

Nate crumpled to the sidewalk but not before he saw a dark car swerve onto the sidewalk and hit Bliss head-on with such purpose and speed that the mayor's body flew over the hood and landed with a dreadful thump several feet away.

The car's engine roared as it regained the road and

disappeared up the highway, leaving Mayor Bliss's body in its wake.

Nate closed his eyes as the world drifted away.

Epilogue

One Month Later

The sun felt great coming through the windshield, the breeze from the open window warm and welcoming. Sarah checked the rearview mirror as she did every few minutes, just to make sure the horse trailer was where it was supposed to be, fastened to the back of her new truck, Skipjack safe and secure and on his way to his new home in Arizona.

She then glanced over at her passenger and saw he'd woken up from drifting off somewhere in Nevada. The past month in the hospital had robbed his skin of its light tan, but that would come back, as would his strength. She would make sure of that.

"Where are we?" he asked, stretching his long legs, then wincing as the movement hurt his still mending wounds. He'd almost died four weeks ago, and in fact, if it hadn't been for the slight cushioning impact of her father's leather notebook, which Nate had carried in his jacket, he probably wouldn't be sitting here.

"About two hours from your place," she told him.

"What do you think of Arizona?" he asked.

"It's beautiful."

He waited a second before following his question with

another. "Think you could go to school and live here?" he asked, his hand coming to rest on her thigh.

She looked over from the straight road ahead and smiled. "I think it's possible."

"Yeah, me, too," he said softly, gently squeezing her leg.

She glanced at him again. "You haven't heard from Alex's wife lately, have you?"

"Not for a while. From what I gather, there's been no sign of him anywhere. If he's still alive, he must be somewhere no one expected him to be, either injured or snowed in. I can't believe I wasn't able to help look for him."

"I know it's been gut-wrenching," she said.

"Yeah. Well, a lot of things have been gut-wrenching lately, right?"

"Yes. Don't think less of me, Nate, but I have to admit I'm glad someone killed Bliss. I don't know who it was or what the motive was or anything else. I'm just glad Bliss is history."

"You have every right to feel that way," he said, his voice kind, but she knew he worried about the who and why aspects of Bliss's murder. "The man was behind killing at least four kids as well as your father and Stew Netters," he added.

"And Morris Denton."

"Gallant doesn't think so."

"But Denton was found overdosed in his motel room the same day Netters died."

"There's no proof to link Bliss to that motel room. Besides, drugs seem to be kind of outside his operational pattern. He was more of a 'shoot now, ask questions later' kind of guy. And since his secretary disappeared soon after Bliss's death, there's just a paucity of information. Too bad he burned a bunch of papers before he left."

"Maybe Denton accidentally killed himself."

"Maybe," Nate agreed. "The important thing is B-Strong has been seized by federal agents, and law-enforcement agencies are ratcheting up antiterrorist investigations in the hope of ferreting out other militia groups."

"That is important, but equally so, at least to me, is that you and I survived," Sarah said as she cast him a loving look. "I have something to tell you," she added.

Nate looked over at her. "Yeah?"

"Open my purse and take out the paper inside."

He did as she'd asked. "This is one of those letters, isn't it? One that Johnny wrote you before you were married."

"Yes. Read it. Out loud, I mean. Please."

He cleared his throat. "'Baby,'" he began, and in some odd way, he sounded a little like Johnny. "'Baby, don't cry. I promised you that I would marry you and that hasn't changed. I know losing the baby hurts and I know your dad celebrating the miscarriage hurts even more. But you belong with me now, Sarah, and together, we'll have a bunch of kids, as many as you want. So don't cry. Nothing has changed. Love, Johnny.'"

Nate lowered the letter and took a deep breath. "Well, now I see why you loved him so much," he said.

She blinked a couple of times. "Yes. Well, I always fall in love with really good men. Both times now. It's like I've got a gift for it."

"I'm sorry you lost the baby," he added.

"Thank you for saying that. It was really early in the pregnancy, but I guess that doesn't matter sometimes. Dad was overjoyed. He told Johnny to get lost and made plans to send me to live with an aunt in Alaska. My mom had flitted off to who knows where by then. What Dad couldn't wrap his head around was that Johnny and I wanted that baby. It hadn't been planned, but from the moment we knew, everything just changed. It was a tragedy to lose it, not the blessing Dad claimed it was, and it broke my heart."

"Did you try again?" he asked softly.

"No. There was school and work and loans. And I was afraid. You know. And then it was too late. He was dead."

She saw a rest stop ahead and pulled off the road, parking the rig in the shade of a big tree. By unspoken agreement, she and Nate both got out of the truck and met in the front. He took her hand and led her to a picnic table, where they sat side by side on the table itself, their feet on the bench, their shoulders and hips touching. The sun beat down on their heads. To Sarah it felt as though the rays infused themselves right into her bones, spreading light and warmth through her body.

"I love you, Sarah," he said, gripping her hand and looking into her eyes. "I have from the beginning and I don't see it ever changing. But if I learned anything in this last month or so it's this—I'm born to be in law enforcement, on the front lines, taking care of business. As soon as I get home I'll tell my boss I want my badge back. I know it's a lot to ask of you, but do you think you could handle being married to another cop?"

She smiled as she stared at their interlocked fingers. "I know who you are, Nate. I would never want you to be anything or anyone else."

"Ditto," he said. A moment later, he added, "So, you will marry me someday? You'll have our babies?"

She nodded, too emotional to speak.

The smile started in his eyes, then spread to his lips, and the next thing she knew, he'd wrapped her in his arms. Wounded or not wounded, he held her so close she wasn't sure where he stopped and she began. And when he kissed her, the sensation of their bodies and lives merging into one completely overwhelmed her.

Whatever the future held, they would face it together. Always.

* * * * *

*Don't miss Alice Sharpe's STRANDED,
the second book in her miniseries*
THE RESCUERS, *on sale next month.
Look for it wherever
Harlequin Intrigue books are sold!*

COMING NEXT MONTH FROM

H HARLEQUIN®

I N T R I G U E®

Available June 17, 2014

#1503 WEDDING AT CARDWELL RANCH
Cardwell Cousins • by B.J. Daniels
Someone is hell-bent on making Allie Taylor think she's losing her mind. Allie's past has stalked her to Cardwell Ranch, and not even Jackson Cardwell may be able to save her from a killer with a chilling agenda.

#1504 HARD RIDE TO DRY GULCH
Big "D" Dads: The Daltons • by Joanna Wayne
Faith Ashburn turns to sexy detective Travis Dalton to find and save her missing son. In the process, will Travis lose his heart and find a family?

#1505 UNDERCOVER WARRIOR
Copper Canyon • by Aimée Thurlo
Was Agent Kyle Goodluck's last undercover assignment too close to home for comfort? Now Kyle's only hope to prevent an attack that would rock the entire nation is the mysterious woman he's just rescued from terrorists, Erin Barrett.

#1506 EXPLOSIVE ENGAGEMENT
Shotgun Weddings • by Lisa Childs
Stacy Kozminski and Logan Payne must fake an engagement to survive. But with someone trying to kill them with bullets and bombs, they may never make it to the altar.

#1507 STRANDED
The Rescuers • by Alice Sharpe
When detective Alex Foster returns from the dead, he wants two things: his estranged, pregnant wife, Jessica, to love him, and to capture the man who wants them both dead....

#1508 SANCTUARY IN CHEF VOLEUR
The Delancey Dynasty • by Mallory Kane
Hannah Martin flees to New Orleans looking for help from PI Mack Griffin. It doesn't take him long to appreciate Hannah's courage and resourcefulness, or to realize that he may end up needing protection, too—from his feelings for her. _____

YOU CAN FIND MORE INFORMATION ON UPCOMING HARLEQUIN® TITLES, FREE EXCERPTS AND MORE AT WWW.HARLEQUIN.COM.

HICNM0614

REQUEST YOUR FREE BOOKS!
2 FREE NOVELS PLUS 2 FREE GIFTS!

HARLEQUIN

INTRIGUE

BREATHTAKING ROMANTIC SUSPENSE

YES! Please send me 2 FREE Harlequin Intrigue® novels and my 2 FREE gifts (gifts are worth about $10). After receiving them, if I don't wish to receive any more books, I can return the shipping statement marked "cancel." If I don't cancel, I will receive 6 brand-new novels every month and be billed just $4.74 per book in the U.S. or $5.24 per book in Canada. That's a savings of at least 14% off the cover price! It's quite a bargain! Shipping and handling is just 50¢ per book in the U.S. and 75¢ per book in Canada.* I understand that accepting the 2 free books and gifts places me under no obligation to buy anything. I can always return a shipment and cancel at any time. Even if I never buy another book, the two free books and gifts are mine to keep forever.

182/382 HDN F42N

Name	(PLEASE PRINT)	
Address		Apt. #
City	State/Prov.	Zip/Postal Code

Signature (if under 18, a parent or guardian must sign)

Mail to the **Harlequin® Reader Service:**
IN U.S.A.: P.O. Box 1867, Buffalo, NY 14240-1867
IN CANADA: P.O. Box 609, Fort Erie, Ontario L2A 5X3

**Are you a subscriber to Harlequin Intrigue books
and want to receive the larger-print edition?
Call 1-800-873-8635 or visit www.ReaderService.com.**

* Terms and prices subject to change without notice. Prices do not include applicable taxes. Sales tax applicable in N.Y. Canadian residents will be charged applicable taxes. Offer not valid in Quebec. This offer is limited to one order per household. Not valid for current subscribers to Harlequin Intrigue books. All orders subject to credit approval. Credit or debit balances in a customer's account(s) may be offset by any other outstanding balance owed by or to the customer. Please allow 4 to 6 weeks for delivery. Offer available while quantities last.

Your Privacy—The Harlequin® Reader Service is committed to protecting your privacy. Our Privacy Policy is available online at www.ReaderService.com or upon request from the Harlequin Reader Service.

We make a portion of our mailing list available to reputable third parties that offer products we believe may interest you. If you prefer that we not exchange your name with third parties, or if you wish to clarify or modify your communication preferences, please visit us at www.ReaderService.com/consumerschoice or write to us at Harlequin Reader Service Preference Service, P.O. Box 9062, Buffalo, NY 14269. Include your complete name and address.

HI13R

Read on for a sneak peek of
WEDDING AT CARDWELL RANCH
by New York Times *bestselling author*

B. J. Daniels
Part of the CARDWELL COUSINS series.

In Montana for his brother's nuptials,
Jackson Cardwell isn't looking to be anybody's hero.
But the Texas single father knows a beautiful lady in
distress when he meets her.

"I'm afraid to ask what you just said to your horse," Jackson joked
as he moved closer. Her horse had wandered over to some tall grass
away from the others.

"Just thanking him for not bucking me off," she admitted shyly.

"Probably a good idea, but your horse is a she. A mare."

"Oh, hopefully she wasn't insulted." Allie actually smiled. The
afternoon sun lit her face along with the smile.

He felt his heart do a loop-de-loop. He tried to rein it back in as he
looked into her eyes. That tantalizing green was deep and dark, inviting,
and yet he knew a man could drown in those eyes.

Suddenly, Allie's horse shied. In the next second it took off as if it
had been shot from a cannon. To her credit, she hadn't let go of her reins,
but she grabbed the saddle horn and let out a cry as the mare raced out
of the meadow headed for the road.

Jackson spurred his horse and raced after her. He could hear the
startled cries of the others behind him. He'd been riding since he was a
boy, so he knew how to handle his horse. But Allie, he could see, was
having trouble staying in the saddle with her horse at a full gallop.

He pushed his horse harder and managed to catch her, riding
alongside until he could reach over and grab her reins. The horses
lunged along for a moment. Next to him Allie started to fall. He grabbed
for her, pulling her from her saddle and into his arms as he released her

reins and brought his own horse up short.

Allie slid down his horse to the ground. He dismounted and dropped beside her. "Are you all right?"

"I think so. What happened?"

He didn't know. One minute her horse was munching on grass, the next it had taken off like a shot.

Allie had no idea why the horse had reacted like that. She hated that she was the one who'd upset everyone.

"Are you sure you didn't spur your horse?" Natalie asked, still upset.

"She isn't wearing spurs," Ford pointed out.

"Maybe a bee stung your horse," Natalie suggested.

Dana felt bad. "I wanted your first horseback-riding experience to be a pleasant one," she lamented.

"It was. It is," Allie reassured her, although in truth, she wasn't looking forward to getting back on the horse. But she knew she had to for Natalie's sake. The kids had been scared enough as it was.

Dana had spread out the lunch on a large blanket with the kids all helping when Jackson rode up, trailing her horse. The mare looked calm now, but Allie wasn't sure she would ever trust it again.

Jackson met her gaze as he dismounted. Dana was already on her feet, heading for him. Allie left the kids to join them.

"What is it?" Dana asked, keeping her voice down.

Jackson looked to Allie as if he didn't want to say in front of her.

"Did I do something to the horse to make her do that?" she asked, fearing that she had.

His expression softened as he shook his head. "You didn't do *anything*." He looked at Dana. "Someone shot the mare."

Someone is hell-bent on making Allie Taylor think she's losing her mind. Jackson's determined to unmask the perp. Can he guard the widowed wedding planner and her little girl from a killer with a chilling agenda?

Find out what happens next in
WEDDING AT CARDWELL RANCH
by New York Times *bestselling author B.J. Daniels,*
available July 2014, only from Harlequin® Intrigue®.

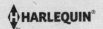

INTRIGUE®

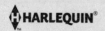